# The Gracie Jones Chronicles: Visiting the Vanderbilts

*A Novel by*
*Catherine McGrew Jaime*

**Other Historical Fiction by Catherine Jaime**

*Leonardo the Florentine*
*Leonardo: Masterpieces in Milan*
*Leonardo: To Mantua and Beyond*
*Leonardo: A Return to Florence*
*Failure in Philadelphia?*
*York Proceeded On*
*The Attack in Cappadocia*
*The Attack at Shkodra*
*The Attack on Wuerzburg*

## Creative Learning Connection

8006 Old Madison Pike, Ste 11-A
Madison, Alabama 35758
U.S.A.
www.CreativeLearningConnection.com

# Preface

I fell in love with the Biltmore home and the corresponding stories of the George Vanderbilt family when I first visited the house during the spring of 2014. That first weekend visit quickly became multiple visits, numerous tours of the house, and hundreds of hours of research into the lives of those who had built and lived in this amazing place.

As a historian, it is always important to me that my historical novels are as accurate as possible. But as a story teller I also want to tell a good story. My hope is that I have accomplished both. The story is told from the point of view of a fictional character, a friend of Cornelia Vanderbilt, the 12-year-old daughter of George and Edith Vanderbilt. Gracie gives us the perspective of an outsider looking in at the amazing family that made the Biltmore what it was and contributed to what it is today. She gives us the chance to see how one of the richest families in the country lived in this era just beyond the Gilded Age. She describes for us the servants and the grandeur she sees, but also helps us see beyond all that, as she surely would have had to, to see the real people who lived those lives.

The lives of even the wealthiest were not without pain and death. This story doesn't dwell on those things, but it does introduce the anguish that even the wealthiest can feel at the death of a servant, a cousin, and in this case, ultimately, a father. I had considered ending the novel before the death of George Vanderbilt, but the story didn't seem complete. In the third and final section, the girls discuss the sudden death of Cornelia's father, which had occurred shortly after Gracie's second visit to Asheville. They don't dwell on it, but I felt mention had to be made.

Even if you are not a 12-year-old girl, I hope you can let yourself enjoy this story! May it bring you a little closer to the Vanderbilts in the process; and, to an even greater appreciation of what George Washington Vanderbilt accomplished with the Biltmore.

# Chapter One

Gracie stretched out on the bed again, Cornelia's letter in her hand. She missed her friend when the Vanderbilts traveled abroad, but at least Cornelia was good about writing letters to her when they were away.

Gracie turned the page and read the letter again, smiling at the stories Cornelia told of her family motoring across Europe, "Gracie, the thrill is almost too hard to describe as we speed from place to place. It makes me never want to travel by carriage again." Gracie tried to imagine the Vanderbilts all decked out in their motoring clothes and laughed at the thought.

Cornelia had continued, "We have tickets to return to the United States next month on the *Titanic*. I cannot wait to see the luxurious ship that has been so much in the news recently. Daddy says our suites are to be quite large and quite lovely. It is practically a floating palace."

Gracie laughed again. The *Titanic* must really be something if even the Vanderbilts could feel at home aboard it.

Gracie put the letter down and daydreamed about traveling on such a marvelous ship. She had even heard that it had grand staircases and chandeliers and orchestras and, why, everything. *Yes, the Vanderbilts should feel right at home,* she thought again. Gracie wasn't really envious of her friend and the outrageously large house she lived in or the trips overseas that she and her family took each year. She really wasn't.

Slowly Gracie shook her head. No, that wasn't true. She was a little jealous. Not so much of the mansion that sounded like it was the size of a small city, or the countless servants who Cornelia described as if they were everywhere in the house. But, yes, the annual trips abroad did make her more than a little green. In twelve short years Cornelia had been more places and seen more parts of Europe than most adults, at least the adults that Gracie knew. But she herself would probably never travel beyond New York City and the City of Washington. Oh well, she would be content. If she was going to be stuck in one place all her life, what better place to live than the grand city of New York?

~^~

Gracie had not meant to fall asleep, but she awoke some time later with a start. She realized she had been dreaming of the boarding school in Washington where she and Cornelia had met two years earlier. It had always seemed to both girls that their friendship had been ordained. How else could anyone explain how the two of them had ended up at the same boarding school in the City of Washington on the same day to determine if they would attend it? Especially since neither of them had ended up attending the school – though for two entirely different reasons: Gracie's parents had decided that they just couldn't afford the school after all. Gracie was fairly sure the Vanderbilts could have bought the school, so expenses hadn't deterred them. No, the Vanderbilts had chosen not to send Cornelia after reconsidering their schedules. Committing to the school's calendar would have put too much of a crimp in their annual travel plans. Gracie had heard that at some point in the future they might send Cornelia, but for now they had chosen the small school they had founded in Asheville and tutors at their estate. Gracie had also heard that Mr. Vanderbilt's pre-university education had all been with tutors, and he didn't seem any worse for it, so she could see why they liked that option for Cornelia.

So, here the girls were two years later, with neither of them having attended the boarding school. But from that casual first meeting the girls had become the closest of friends; even though most of their friendship had developed via letters such as this one.

Gracie smoothed out the letter she had fallen asleep holding. She could hardly contain her excitement. The Vanderbilts had invited her to come to Biltmore next month soon after their return from Europe. They would arrive in New York City in the middle of the month. Maybe she could arrange with her parents to meet them at Chelsea Pier and welcome them back to the United States when the *Titanic* arrived.

Gracie had heard that there would be quite a party put on by the citizens of

New York City to herald the arrival of the *Titanic* at the end of its maiden voyage. Many prominent New Yorkers were scheduled to be aboard, in addition to the Vanderbilts. It would certainly be a momentous occasion to be a part of.

~^~

Gracie busied herself with her chores each day after school, excitedly awaiting the arrival of her friend. Her parents hadn't liked the idea of her being at the pier when the *Titanic* arrived, but her father had finally consented to take her if his schedule allowed. "There will just be too many people there for a young lady to go alone," she could still hear him saying. She didn't mind if he came, too. She just wanted to see this marvelous new ship for herself, as well as getting to see the Vanderbilts again as soon as possible.

# Chapter Two

Gracie held the telegraph in her hand. She didn't know whether to laugh or to cry. She had been so looking forward to the arrival of the *Titanic*, but Cornelia had just sent word that they weren't traveling on it after all. Rather last minute Mr. Vanderbilt had changed his mind and booked passage for them on one of the *Titanic's* sister ships instead; the *Olympic* was returning to the states slightly earlier than the *Titanic*. For some reason, Mr. Vanderbilt had determined that it was time to return home to check on the estate, and make sure the farming operations were all going well.

Gracie had no difficulty imagining Mr. Vanderbilt making the decision that it was time to return to his estate as spring was arriving. In her limited conversations with him over the last two years she could tell that he loved to be working at his estate as much as he loved traveling.

With the last minute change to the Vanderbilts' arrival schedule, Gracie knew her father wouldn't be likely to find the time to take her to meet them. She would have to be content with seeing them at Biltmore in a few weeks.

~^~

On their arrival day Gracie found herself lounging around, trying not to be depressed at having to wait to see her friend. She was glad her mother had allowed her to go to her room after she returned from school, rather than joining her younger siblings in their chores. Gracie sighed as she stared at her ceiling. *I guess I've lived this long without seeing Cornelia, what's a few more weeks?* she thought miserably.

Rolling to her side and staring at her wall, Gracie didn't hear her father walk in behind her. She almost jumped off the bed when he stood behind her and pretended to be impatient with her. "Let's go, girl," he fussed.

Gracie turned around, clearly surprised. "Oh Papa, you did make it home. I'll grab my shoes quickly and tell Mama that I'm leaving."

Gracie was off the bed and ready to leave before her father could consider changing his mind. The two of them made their way to Chelsea Pier, with Gracie trying unsuccessfully not to talk incessantly during their entire walk. It had been too long since she had last seen Cornelia, since just before they had headed to Europe so many months ago. It was abundantly clear to Mr. Jones that his daughter was having difficulty containing her excitement to be seeing Cornelia again. He listened patiently, glad that his daughter was so excited and pleased that he had been able to get home early enough to take her.

As they got closer to the docks, Gracie's excitement was almost impossible to contain. The *Olympic* seemed to tower over them as they approached it. Father and daughter stood amongst the throngs of others waiting to welcome home family and friends who had traveled abroad.

Gracie wondered how they would ever spot the Vanderbilts amongst so many people. Then she realized that the fancier-dressed people were all coming off the same gangway. "Come on Papa, let's move further this direction. I think the Vanderbilts will come down over here."

She practically dragged her father forward, so afraid that they might miss the Vanderbilts. Suddenly she realized her concerns were unwarranted. With Mrs. Vanderbilt being almost six feet tall and Mr. Vanderbilt being over six feet, they were actually easy to spot as they started their descent towards land.

"Papa, Papa, there they are," Gracie squealed. She almost lost contact with her father as she surged forward, but he pulled her back gently. "They will have to walk right past us where we are. Please give them a couple of minutes to get their feet on the ground."

Gracie consented, and tried to wait patiently for the Vanderbilts to arrive in front of them. Cornelia finally spotted Gracie. She practically ran down the remainder of the gangway into her arms. "Gracie, I've missed you so much."

Eventually Mr. and Mrs. Vanderbilt made their way down to the little group. Mr. Jones put out his hand. "Mr. Vanderbilt, how nice to see you again."

While the grownups exchanged their greetings, the girls talked excitedly. It didn't take long before Cornelia could be heard saying, "Daddy, Gracie should go to Biltmore with us now instead of coming down in a few weeks. Please, Daddy, please."

Mr. Jones started to protest that the school year wasn't quite over, when Mr. Vanderbilt took him aside. The girls strained to hear their conversation, and Cornelia looked pleadingly at her mother for support.

After what seemed an insufferable amount of time, both fathers returned to the ladies smiling. Mr. Jones spoke first. "Mr. Vanderbilt has assured me that you can attend the local school with Cornelia when you first get to Biltmore. But you must promise me that you will not slack off on your school work just because you are away."

Gracie grinned excitedly and Mr. Vanderbilt addressed both girls. "It will be a week or so before we've finished in New York City. We have family to catch up with, and I have some business matters to attend to. When we have a better idea of our departure date, we will contact you and arrange to pick Gracie up before we go to the train station."

# Chapter Three

It was still going to be a few days before the Vanderbilts picked her up, but Gracie was anxious to begin her packing. It wasn't as if she really had that much to take with her. Fortunately Cornelia had already informed her that they could share clothes during Gracie's visit, though Gracie realized she had little to contribute to the sharing. But she could at least bring a few of her personal items and some of her favorite clothes. Cornelia had also hinted that she should leave room in her trunk for extra things on her return trip. Gracie didn't spend much time worrying about what Cornelia meant by that; she didn't really have enough to fill a trunk anyway.

Gracie was in the process of deciding on a few last things when her younger sister Beth came into the room looking like she was going to cry. Gracie had really thought her sister would be happy to see her gone for a while, so that she would get the chance to fill the role of big sister. But from the look on Beth's face, Gracie guessed that wasn't the case.

Gracie put down the two skirts she had been trying to choose between and hugged her sister. "I'm not leaving quite yet. Why don't we play a game as soon as I'm done packing? I've heard that the Vanderbilts have a fabulous chess set and you know Cornelia is likely to beat me at every game. You can go get our chess set out and we can get in a few practice games."

Beth smiled at Gracie's suggestion. She was better at chess than her older sister, and was always up to a game to prove it!

After the packing had been completed, Gracie and Beth played several games of chess and were helping Mama with dinner preparations when Papa arrived home. He held a newspaper in his hand and looked pale. He brought the newspaper to the table and spread it out for all to see. The headlines of the New York Times practically screamed the terrible news:

"TITANIC SINKS FOUR HOURS AFTER HITTING ICEBERG; 866

RESCUED BY CARPATHIA, PROBABLY 1250 PERISH."

Gracie sank into the nearest chair, her heart and head pounding. The unsinkable Titanic had sunk? The luxury ship that the Vanderbilts had planned to travel home from Europe on? It was difficult to even imagine.

Mama drew closer to the newspaper, reading more of the tragic news out loud with a strained voice. As she read the news of the loss of many of the second and third class passengers, she turned the job of reading over to Papa, and joined Gracie, who was seated in a chair at the table. When Papa had read the remainder of the newspaper article aloud, all stood or sat quietly for a few moments. Papa finally broke the silence, "We should pray for the families who lost loved ones on that ship, and those who are still awaiting word one way or another." Gracie closed her eyes, joining her family in prayer and adding a prayer of thanksgiving that the Vanderbilts had been spared. She wondered how they were taking the news of the tragedy.

# Chapter Four

On departure day, word came that the Vanderbilts would be spending a few hours at the Metropolitan Museum of Art before they headed to the train station. Could Gracie be ready early and join them? Gracie laughed; she had been packed for days and had just been counting down the days and hours until departure time.

A short time later, after saying her goodbyes to the family, Gracie stepped out of her house and towards the most magnificent carriage she had ever seen.

"Come, sit up here by me, Gracie," Cornelia offered. "We came a bit earlier because Daddy said we could go for a carriage ride through Central Park before we went to the art museum. I hope you don't mind."

Gracie shook her head. How could she possibly mind? She had seen the carriages that sauntered through Central Park on many of her trips through the park with her family, but she had never even dared to imagine being able to ride in one.

Gracie had trouble catching her breath as they rode through the New York City streets in the magnificent carriage. She had never seen the city from this angle. She had walked miles and miles of city streets, of course, and taken the occasional street car ride with one or both of her parents. But a carriage? It was simply too amazing.

Cornelia ignored the city sights as they rode; watching her friend's excitement was much more fun. Before it seemed possible they had ridden through much of Central Park and the carriage was dropping them in front of the Metropolitan.

Mr. and Mrs. Vanderbilt had already told the girls where to meet them at the front of the museum when their allotted time was up. Getting down from the carriage, the girls raced to the top of the steps. Standing at the top, Gracie enjoyed one last look at the park before entering the building. She squeezed Cornelia's hand and whispered an appreciative thank you.

With all her trips to the Met with her family, Gracie didn't think any had been more delightful than this time with Cornelia was going to be. They entered the museum hand in hand, both anticipating what they would get to see again. They should have time to stroll through most of the galleries, as long as they didn't take too long in any one room. Besides, Gracie had been to the Metropolitan often enough with her family that she had already decided it would be okay if they didn't make it to every room on this visit.

Her family often came on Sunday afternoons even when they only had an hour to spend. On those occasions they walked through just one portion of the museum, with her parents passing on stories of many of the artists or paintings as they went. It had always seemed to Gracie to be the best way to spend a Sunday afternoon. But, now to have several hours here with Cornelia, that would be a unique treat.

The girls entered the first gallery together but immediately got split up. Cornelia had spotted one of her favorite paintings across the room and made a beeline for it. Gracie made her way carefully around the room, taking a quick glance at each painting before stopping in front of Cornelia's favorite with her. Then they were off to the next room to repeat the process, with both girls thoroughly enjoying the experience. Periodically they would stop and discuss a piece that they both found fascinating.

After making their way through much of the rest of the museum, both girls concurred that the European Paintings section was their favorite part. They stopped together in an area with Dutch paintings and Gracie clapped her hands in joy. "I love both of these paintings of vases with flowers, don't you, Cornelia?"

Cornelia shrugged. "I see real vases of flowers equally as beautiful every day at home. I'm not really sure why anyone would pay good money for paintings of them."

Gracie snorted and turned her back to her friend. "I just can't decide which one I like best, the one by Jacob Vosmaer or the one by Margareta Haverman. They are both so colorful, and really just so beautiful, no matter what you say, Cornelia."

Cornelia shrugged her shoulders. "We can agree to disagree. But if I was choosing between the two I would definitely choose the one by Margareta."

Gracie turned back towards her friend a little, "Oh, do you like that one better?"

"Not necessarily. I just like that it was done by a woman. We are certainly not seeing very many paintings here by women artists, are we?"

Gracie had to agree that they had been pretty rare. "While I think that's a good point, I still like both of them."

Cornelia grabbed her hand. "Let's find something besides flowers to look at."

As they came around the corner into a room with Italian art, Gracie started giggling. "Do you like this type of still life any better?" she asked.

Cornelia turned to see the painting Gracie was pointing at. "A cat and dead fish? Yuck. Okay, you win, the flowers in the vases were nicer."

But beyond the cat still life Cornelia spotted a smaller painting she did actually like. "Look, Gracie, a painting by the Venetian painter, Giovanni Battista Tiepolo. This is the kind of painting I like to see, where he uses the architecture to showcase the people. It actually looks like something is happening here; like it's telling a story."

Both girls stood in front of the painting, enjoying the details of it together. But as they walked away, Gracie just had to ask, "Does your father collect paintings of still life, Cornelia?"

Cornelia laughed. "No I'm pretty sure most of our paintings are of people – usually real people. Though you really won't find that many paintings at our house, Daddy likes to collect engravings more than paintings. When I was little we had more paintings, but Daddy sold most of them a long time ago. Personally I like paintings better."

The girls continued through the European paintings, excited to be looking at them together even when they disagreed. Walking into one of the French rooms, Cornelia suddenly exclaimed excitedly, "Look Gracie it's a Renoir. Don't you just love Renoir?"

Gracie stood in front of the large painting. "I don't think I've ever seen a Renoir besides this one. The family in it is quite lovely, though the style is quite different than the others we've been looking at."

"Oh, Gracie, I just love the modern, impressionist works. But, wait until we get home. Daddy owns two very lovely Renoirs that I can't wait to show you. He bought them on one of his many trips to France. They are much smaller than this one, but I'm sure you will like them, too."

As the girls continued through a little more of the museum, they suddenly realized that it was time to meet Mr. and Mrs. Vanderbilt. "We better hurry," Gracie exclaimed, "we shouldn't be late to meet your parents after all they've done."

Cornelia didn't look particularly concerned, but finally nodded in agreement. "I guess that would be a bad start to your trip, yes, let's go quickly to the front."

They reconnected with Mr. and Mrs. Vanderbilt in the foyer, talking over each other as they both tried to tell them what they had seen. Mr. and Mrs. Vanderbilt exchanged glances. It was clear that the visit to the Metropolitan had been a good end to their time in New York City.

# Chapter Five

A private car awaited them in front of the museum and they were ferried across the city to the train station, where Gracie was introduced to a new level of luxury – the Vanderbilts' private railway car, the *Swannanoa*. Gracie tried to take in her luxurious surroundings as she was ushered to her seat. *So much to see,* she thought. As she looked around, Gracie wondered if Mr. Vanderbilt had designed the car.

The girls sat next to each other as the train moved along at an increasingly rapid speed. Gracie tried to look at the scenery while still talking incessantly. Mr. and Mrs. Vanderbilt looked on in amusement, wondering how two twelve-year-olds could find so much to talk about.

Cornelia tried to fill her friend in on all the things they would do on her visit to Biltmore – from horseback riding and swimming, to fancy dinners every night.

Mr. Vanderbilt leaned over at one point and held his hand up. "Remember girls, all that will have to wait until school is over. I promised Mr. Jones that Gracie would finish out this year's studies."

The two girls groaned simultaneously. Then they both shrugged and went back to their conversation. Mr. Vanderbilt smiled as he watched the girls. He was content with the friend his young daughter had made. Quietly he leaned over to Mrs. Vanderbilt, "Miss Gracie seems to have a good head on her shoulders. I think she and Cornelia will play well together this summer."

Mrs. Vanderbilt stifled a laugh and whispered back, "I don't think at their age they call it playing, dear. But yes, she should be a pleasant addition to the family over the next few months."

Both parents leaned back and continued to watch the girls with their animated conversations. It was fun to see the enthusiasm both girls showed as they made their plans. Yes, it would be good to have a companion for Cornelia for a while.

When Cornelia had first invited her to join them for their trip to Asheville, Gracie had wondered why the Vanderbilts hadn't driven between Asheville and New York City, since she had heard that they owned at least one automobile on both sides of the Atlantic. The stories of the family motoring across Germany had made it clear to her that traveling by automobile was enjoyable to them. But watching Cornelia's parents sitting comfortably across from her in the midst of all this luxury she thought she might be able to understand.

As Gracie pondered it, Cornelia leaned over and mentioned how comfortable riding in the *Swannanoa* always seemed to her. "Is this why your family travels by train when you come to New York City, because of how luxurious the *Swannanoa* is?" Gracie asked, hoping the question didn't sound rude.

Cornelia smiled. "No, I think it's the other way around. I think Daddy designed the *Swannanoa* to be so comfortable because we always travel by train when we can. I think it has something to do with loyalty."

Gracie look at Cornelia quizzically and she continued. "Daddy says

Vanderbilt money comes from railroads, and has for many, many years. As a result I think most of Daddy's family members travel by train when they can."

Gracie was surprised. *I thought Papa said the Vanderbilts were investors. But I guess Cornelia should know, it's her family.* Gracie settled into the comfortable seat, content to travel in such style, regardless of the reason. *I don't know when I'll ever get to do this again,* she mused. *I should certainly enjoy it.*

After a few moments of pleasant silence the girls went back to talking about what lay ahead. "If you think the *Swannanoa* is luxurious, wait until you see our home, Gracie. Daddy did such a great job designing it. I can't wait for you to see it. It is simply enormous, with hundreds and hundreds of rooms."

Gracie smiled to herself, sure that even a Vanderbilt couldn't have a house with hundreds of rooms. Cornelia continued to describe the house with great enthusiasm, and Gracie tried to pick out which things Cornelia was exaggerating about. "And of course you will just adore the artwork. I think Daddy has art on every wall of the house."

Gracie nodded, quite confident that Mr. Vanderbilt at least had more art than anyone else she knew personally. Art was what had connected her and Cornelia two years before when they had first met, and probably the one thing that connected their two families. *It isn't money, that's for sure,* Gracie thought to herself, looking around the car they were traveling in again. *I'm pretty sure more money was spent on the decorations for this car than my family has ever spent on anything.* She looked again at the sumptuous furniture and the gilded frames around both art and mirrors. *Yes, this car is truly a work of art in and of itself.*

~^~

At some point during their travels Gracie realized that Cornelia had fallen asleep. Gracie passed some time looking out the windows of the car at the passing scenery, her thoughts turning abruptly back to the *Titanic* tragedy. She wondered again how the Vanderbilts felt about it. *Do they appreciate how close they came to being on it? Did they know any of the others who had perished?* She thought it would be rude or insensitive to bring up the topic, so she told herself she would try to avoid thinking about it too much during the visit. *If Cornelia wants to speak of it, I will let her bring the subject up*, she told herself, *but otherwise, I certainly will not.*

# Chapter Six

After two enjoyable days of train travel, the small group arrived in Asheville. Gracie realized she had never been this far south before. A carriage from the estate was waiting at the train station and the girls jumped into a seat almost simultaneously. After a warning look from her mother, Cornelia moved so that Gracie could have the side with the best view of the mountains. Gracie gasped as the Blue Ridge Mountains opened up in her view. "Cornelia, they are so beautiful. And so big. I had never imagined."

Gracie struggled to see everything on both sides as they rode on. She tried to imagine what the Vanderbilt home would look like after all this. A home? Yes, she reminded herself, even if it was the size of a large European castle, it was still the home of Cornelia and her parents.

Gracie realized suddenly that the carriage had slowed down as it prepared to turn onto a smaller road. She looked about as they passed by a small gate house and under a beautiful stone arch. *We must have entered the estate property,* she thought.

Just then Mr. and Mrs. Vanderbilt squeezed together and motioned for Gracie to join them on the seat opposite hers and Cornelia's. "Here, you'll have a better view of the approach road and the chateau from this side."

Gracie took them up on their generous offer, enjoying seeing the variety of plants that grew along the winding road. Noticing her delight Mr. Vanderbilt explained, "Mr. Olmsted planted all of those, and the majority of the trees you are seeing to both sides of us. This was mostly open farmland when I purchased it."

Gracie nodded, amazed at all that had been done around her. "I know that name, but I don't know why. Would I have heard of Mr. Olmsted before?" she asked.

"Oh yes, undoubtedly," Mrs. Vanderbilt responded. "Mr. Olmsted was one of the primary planners for Central

Park, along with Mr. Hunt, another name you will likely hear often during your visit." She smiled, looking knowingly at her husband. She knew full well how proud he was of his accomplishments at Biltmore, but also that he willingly shared the credit with the two men who had most assisted in making his dream a reality.

Gracie continued to look in both directions as often as she could, in awe over the size of the property they had already ridden through. But she still was not prepared for what lay ahead when the carriage went through a delicate wrought iron gate almost an hour later. As the carriage stopped on the other side of the gate, she saw the biggest, best manicured lawn she had ever seen, topped by a house so enormous she could barely take it in.

Cornelia grabbed her hand. "Let's get out here. You can see the house better if we walk the rest of the way."

Gracie nodded, feeling suddenly speechless, and exited the carriage with her friend. They stood side by side looking across the lawn at the house.

Gracie finally found a few words. "It is simply enormous, Cornelia. I don't think you were kidding about there being hundreds of rooms."

Cornelia laughed. "Of course not. I believe the actual count is two hundred fifty rooms, though I could be off by a few one way or another. I don't know if anyone has actually counted them, I know I certainly haven't. Are you up to a full tour today or would you rather wait until tomorrow?"

Gracie couldn't even begin to imagine how long a tour of the entire house would take. "Maybe we could just do one floor today?" she asked tentatively, really wanting to see the entire house, but not sure that she could muster that much energy after two long days of travel. *Even traveling in comfortable accommodations is exhausting,* she realized.

"Well, then we'll start on the second floor. I'll you show you my bedroom, and your bedroom, which is right next door, of course. And the Living Hall and whichever guest rooms are currently unoccupied. Oh, and I'll introduce you to Anne if we see her."

Gracie was confused. "Who's Anne?" she asked, surprised.

"One of our female servants. Didn't I tell you about her? She's a sweetie. You'll like her."

Gracie still didn't understand, but assumed it would become clearer when she met Anne.

As they talked, the girls moved closer to the house and Gracie realized it was even more imposing, and yet even more beautiful, the closer they got to it. She could easily have stood outside gawking at it, but Cornelia dragged her forward, taking her quickly between two stone lions, past two large black wrought iron doors and through the largest front doors Gracie had ever seen.

"Well, would you rather go the second floor via the elevator or the grand staircase?" Cornelia asked. Not waiting for an answer, she moved Gracie towards the elevator.

"Have you ridden in one of these before, Gracie? Mr. Hunt included three of them in the plans for the house; there's even one just for the servants to use. I usually just use the stairs, but since we're tired, let's go in style."

Gracie watched in wonder as the elevator slowly moved them from the first to the second floor. She had heard of elevators in some of the new skyscrapers in New York City, but it had never occurred to her that people might need one in their own homes.

Stepping out of the elevator Gracie looked around in awe. She was already seeing several of the engravings that she had been hearing about from Cornelia. And in front of them was what looked to be a combination sitting room and library. The two girls stepped into the room and Gracie searched the room with her eyes. "Look at all these books, Cornelia. This could be my favorite room in the house. Does your father mind if we read some of them?"

Cornelia shook her head, "No, of course not, that's why they're here. But, I don't think this will be your favorite room, Gracie, I think the Library will be. Maybe we should go see our rooms and then go down there instead of seeing the rest of this floor. The guest rooms aren't going anywhere."

Gracie looked around, clearly confused. "Wait, isn't this the Library?"

Cornelia shook her head again. "Oh no, dear. This is merely a sitting room with some books. Up above us is another sitting room with even more books and the actual library is back downstairs. Right over here are our rooms, let me show you those and then we'll go downstairs and see some real books."

Cornelia took Gracie by the hand and into a doorway across from the sitting room. Trying to take in all the luxury, Gracie was fairly sure a princess would feel right at home in the room. Cornelia took her through another door to a connecting room. "This will officially be your room." Cornelia looked around, and then whispered, "But I'm planning to have the governess sleep in here and you can have her bed in my room. Won't that be more fun?"

Gracie nodded, fairly sure she had never even dreamed of living in such luxury. In one corner of the second room a young woman in a sharp gingham uniform was situating Gracie's trunk. "Oh good, I was hoping you would be around. Gracie, this is Anne; Anne will be your lady's maid while you are at Biltmore. Anne, this is Miss Gracie."

Gracie looked at her friend in surprise. A lady's maid? She decided to ask Cornelia about that surprise announcement later, rather than in front of Anne.

Anne turned to Gracie, doing a slight curtsy. "Miss Gracie, I was just going to unpack your trunk and then have it stored in the trunk room. And then I will be back before dinner to help you with your dress. But if you need something before then, just call me." Anne pointed to a small box on the wall that Gracie was sure she wouldn't have even noticed. Now she saw that it had a small button that she was apparently supposed to push in such an event. Gracie nodded politely, though for the life of her she couldn't figure out what she could possibly need.

Cornelia looked ready to move on, and Gracie took one last look at the room that would be her home for the next few months. It was still hard to imagine living in such luxury.

Gracie followed her friend back out of the bedroom. Cornelia took her back through the sitting room, but this time she led her towards the spiral staircase. "We did the elevator, let's just use the stairs now. I like to see how fast I can run down them, at least as long as there are no guests also using them." She giggled and Gracie imagined that she had not always been so careful. As they descended the beautiful staircase Gracie tried to take in the various paintings they were passing and the beautiful chandelier that hung in the middle of the staircase. It seemed to go on forever, from the first floor up towards the sky, and Gracie wondered how many flights of stairs there were in this amazing place.

As they descended the last steps she finally asked Cornelia about Anne. "A lady's maid? For me? Why?"

Cornelia laughed. "You've obviously never tried to get in and out of the exquisite dresses we get to wear each night for dinner. I'm not sure that you could do that by yourself even if you had a second set of arms. We can help each other if need be, of course, but it's really easier if we each have a lady's maid to help with our hair and our dresses."

Gracie was still laughing as she tried to picture the difficulty of getting dressed and undressed from clothes like the ones Cornelia usually wore. "No I guess I've never worn clothes that required assistance."

Cornelia shrugged and pulled her through a long and narrow room. Several tapestries hung on the left wall and

Gracie tried to stop to admire them. "These are beautiful."

Cornelia slowed her pace, but didn't stop. "Yes, they are some of the fifteenth century Flemish tapestries Daddy bought in Europe. The others are in the Banquet Hall. You can see them this evening at dinner. Come on, I want to show you your soon-to-be-favorite room."

With that, Cornelia pushed open two large wooden doors and led Gracie into the Library.

Gracie gasped. She could hardly believe the quantity of books that surrounded her.

"Oh my, Cornelia. This is truly amazing." With that, Gracie walked around the room slowly, trying to take in all the beautiful volumes in front of her.

"How many books are here? I can't even begin to guess."

Cornelia looked around and tried to answer with a straight face, "Shall we count them? Honestly I don't know for sure, but I've overheard Daddy telling some of his guests that this is about half of his 20,000 books. But, I haven't counted the rooms in this place, I certainly have counted the books."

Gracie and Cornelia looked at each other and laughed at the idea.

"Has he read all of these?" Gracie asked, still trying to take it all in.

"I am sure he hasn't read all of them, but I do know that he has read many of them. He is seldom seen without a book, a magazine, or a newspaper in his hand, so he clearly finds lots of time to read."

Gracie continued to look in awe at the books, wondering if it would be proper to ask to borrow some of the books during her visit.

Cornelia watched her friend for a bit, as if reading her mind. "I'm sure Daddy wouldn't mind you borrowing one or more of his books to read. But, let's save that for later. I'm thinking we will need to be getting ready for dinner soon. Come with me, and we'll choose dresses for dinner."

Gracie followed her friend, already feeling her head spinning with all that there was to see and do at Biltmore. She had stopped paying attention and suddenly realized that Cornelia was carrying on about a parade. "I'm so excited that you arrived at the end of April, Gracie. You'll be able to ride in the

May Celebration Parade with me. Mother and I have ridden in it every year since I was about five years old. Mr. Beadle has one of the gardeners decorate one of our small dainty carriages all over with flowers from our gardens – the horse, the carriage wheels, and why, just everything. Mother told me last year that I was old enough this year to ride without her. So you and I can ride in it together. It will be so much fun."

Gracie nodded, there already seemed to be no shortage of fun in this place, and she had only just arrived.

# Chapter Seven

The next couple of weeks went quickly for Gracie and Cornelia, with much of it spent at school. Gracie especially enjoyed the wagon ride from Biltmore to Asheville each day for school. She loved riding along with Cornelia as they picked up the other children on the estate and then made their way towards town.

*Cornelia may be like the princess of a manor house, but when we go to school she seems just like everybody else,* Gracie thought with pleasure. Still, she was happy as the school term wound down. Cornelia had been anxious for her to really get to experience life at Biltmore, and school had definitely cut into their free time.

But once school was over they were quickly enjoying as many of the outside activities as the two girls could fit into each waking hour. They moved from horseback riding to swimming, from tennis to croquet, and then from archery to shooting practice.

But, as with the other days that had come before, after all that outside fun, it was time to get dressed for the evening meal. Gracie was still enjoying the clothes she had to borrow from Cornelia each night, but did wonder if at some point she would tire of it all. *It's a good thing Cornelia and I are the same size,* she thought. *Otherwise I don't know what I would do. Stay in my room each evening at this time, I suppose.*

Gracie turned to the dress that Anne had laid out on her bed. While waiting for Anne to return to help her, she fingered the beautiful fabric of the long dress. She tried to imagine owning even one such dress, let alone whole closets full of them. *Oh well, I can enjoy the life of a princess while I'm here,* she decided.

After looking herself over in the mirror one more time, Gracie thanked Anne and headed out in search of Cornelia. They almost collided in the hallway outside their rooms.

Both girls giggled and they headed towards the grand staircase to make their grand entrance to the first floor. "Do

you ever get tired of being a princess?"
Gracie had to ask.

Cornelia laughed. "Oh, there are
certainly times I would rather just live in
obscurity somewhere and not be
whispered about as 'a Vanderbilt'
everywhere I go, but in general it's
okay."

Gracie nodded and then
remembered the question she had been
pondering for several days now. "So why
does the food always taste so good here?
My mother is a good cook, but food never
tastes this good at my house."

Cornelia looked around as if she
didn't want anyone to hear the secret.
And then, just for added effect, she
leaned in close to Gracie's ear and
whispered, "It's not your mother's fault."
Laughing, she continued, "I don't think
I've eaten food anywhere in the world
that's as good as it is here at Biltmore.
Most of what we're eating is grown or
raised here on the estate. I think that's
what makes all the difference."

As they entered the Banquet Hall
and were shown their seats by two
sharply dressed servants, Gracie looked
around the room in wonder again,
pondering what Cornelia had just said.

*So it's not the beautiful surroundings of every meal, or the foreign chef, or the big fancy kitchens in the basement, it's as simple as the food being grown here. Well, it makes me feel better about liking it better than what we eat at home. There's not much chance the food we're getting in New York City is this fresh.*

Cornelia waited until the servants had backed away and then turned to Gracie to continue their conversation. "When Daddy and Mr. Hunt started designing the estate here, Daddy wanted it to be self-sufficient, like a European estate. That's part of why he bought so much land. Well, that and he's not a particularly social person. He likes to keep to himself."

Gracie tried to keep from laughing as she looked around the crowded dinner. It seemed that there were dozens of guests almost every night, including artists and authors, politicians and diplomats. And Mr. and Mrs. Vanderbilt sat in the middle of them, laughing and talking about everything from politics to religion to the latest books or the latest opera. She looked at her friend to see if she could possibly have been serious.

It had taken Cornelia a moment to realize how ridiculous her last sentiments had sounded. She tried to keep herself from laughing as she saw Gracie's quizzical look.

"Okay, so maybe that's not quite the right way to put it. I guess it would be better to say he's not a particularly neighborly person. After living so close to so many other people in New York City for so long, he wanted room to do the things he wanted to do, whether it was dance late into the night or take his friends hunting, without having to worry about bothering those around him."

The servants were back, putting a bowl of delicious-smelling vegetable soup in front of the two girls. Cornelia pointed at hers. "As I was saying, this was all grown here. Daddy has farmers here who grow lots of different kinds of fruits and vegetables, and our own chickens and hogs and cattle. And of course the trout come from the two rivers that run through the estate. And, well I guess you get the picture."

Gracie enjoyed the smells of the delicious soup and fresh baked bread before she savored the next course. She tried to decide whether she liked the dinners better here at Biltmore, or the parties that usually came after them. Looking around the crowded Banquet Hall she marveled at how quickly the servants would have all of the dinner dishes cleared away and all other remnants of the meal removed so that the Vanderbilts and their guests could return to the large room for an after dinner dance.

*I hope this is one of the evenings that Mr. and Mrs. Vanderbilt will allow Cornelia and me to return for a portion of the party. I love to hear the music of the singer who has been here this week.*

# Chapter Eight

After many days of outdoor activities throughout the estate, the weather turned very wet very quickly. The girls had been looking for an excuse to curl up in the Library with books since their arrival, and cheerfully changed their plans for the day. Gracie practically skipped down the Tapestry Gallery with glee as she headed back to the Library. She caught her breath as she walked back through the oversized doors into the Library. As if the bookshelves that seemed to cover every square inch of space weren't enough, the room was beautifully decorated, from the lovely wooden floor with its Persian carpets to the beautiful dark fireplace mantle. Gracie had heard that the room had been sized specifically to have room for the Venetian painting that graced the large ceiling of the Library, and from what she had observed of other decisions at the chateau, she was fairly sure the rumor was correct.

Gracie had a sense of anticipation as she walked around the room, longingly looking at the beautifully arranged books. The most difficult part of this first reading session would be choosing – choosing from the many wonderful books in Mr. Vanderbilt's collection. He seemed to have books on every imaginable topic, from architecture to forestry, and from history to philosophy.

Gracie was standing in front of a selection of art books when Cornelia came into the room. Cornelia hugged Gracie and looked in the direction she was looking. "Have you found something of interest already, Gracie?"

Gracie smiled, pointing at the large volumes in front of her. "Actually, before we start reading I would love to look at this set, *Drawings of the Florentine Painters.* Do you think your father would mind?"

Cornelia shook her head. "No, as long as we're careful, he won't mind at all. There's a special slanted table on the other side of the Library. Mr. Hunt designed it mainly for looking at these oversized books. Here, we'll carry the first one over there together."

Both girls leaned down and picked up opposite sides of the oversized volume carefully, slowly maneuvering the heavy book across the room and to the table where they propped the book up on the inclined shelf and carefully opened it.

Gracie had trouble even speaking as they turned to the introduction of the massive book. "May we read this, before we go on?" she found herself whispering.

Cornelia nodded, pleased again to share a love of art with both her parents and her best friend. "I have looked at the drawings in these books several times, but I have never actually read much of it."

Gracie and Cornelia drew close to the book and took turns reading aloud the lengthy introduction. Cornelia smiled when they had finished reading it. "Thank you for suggesting we start with that. I had never realized that Mr. Bernhard had done so much research in compiling these books."

Gracie smiled as Cornelia went on, "I've never asked you why you seem as interested in art as me, Gracie. Art appreciation practically flows through my veins because of my parents and grandparents. But you seem equally at home around great art, which seems..." Cornelia stopped herself, suddenly realizing that her words might come across wrong to her friend.

But Gracie was not bothered by Cornelia's slip. "My parents did not inherit art appreciation quite like yours, but they've lived in New York City all their lives, and have made frequent trips to the Art Museum ever since they married. As we children came along, they started taking us with them. I can remember them pointing out great art to me even before I could read the signs that accompanied the paintings."

Cornelia nodded. She had seen a true sense of understanding in Gracie when they had visited the Metropolitan together. She tried to imagine a whole family going through a museum discussing art. As an only child it was really difficult for her to imagine, but the thought made her smile.

Gracie continued, "I don't know that my younger siblings got the same love of art that I did from our parents, but I certainly follow in their footsteps. In fact, that's one of the many reasons I am enjoying visiting your home – it's like living in an art museum."

Cornelia started to protest Gracie's description, but then looked around the room they were in and laughed instead. "Okay, you win, I guess you could make that comparison."

Gracie hugged her friend. "I don't mean that in a negative way at all. And I would love coming here and spending time with you without all this great art, too, please believe me. But the fact that I can round a corner and face a wall of Dürer prints one moment and go another direction and see paintings by Renoir is a unique and fascinating experience, you must admit."

Cornelia nodded. "Speaking of great art, we should go back to the book or you're going to miss seeing some really great drawings! This volume is okay, but we should finish it, because I really like some of the chapters in the second one – when Mr. Bernhard covers the Renaissance artists of Florence."

With that, both girls turned their attention back to the book, carefully turning each page, reading some of the text, and often stopping to admire the variety of sketches that appeared in front of them. By the time they were finished, they were both exhausted and ready for a break. As Gracie sat back in her chair, Cornelia spoke up, "The rain is letting up some. Let's ring for some refreshments. We can go out on the balcony, sip our lemonade and look out at the mountains in the distance for a little while."

Gracie nodded her approval and both girls skipped out to the balcony, with Cornelia stopping only briefly at the nearest call box to submit their request to the kitchen. A servant had already dried off several of the chairs on the balcony and they sunk contentedly into them, admiring the view.

Gracie pointed in front of them, "Does your family own all of the land that we can see?"

Cornelia nodded. "Yes, pretty much everything. As Daddy mentioned on the trip here, he planted all the trees we can see. Well, not him, personally, of course. But, Daddy followed Mr. Olmsted's suggestions and had hundreds of thousands of trees planted on much of our property. It's hard for me to even imagine how bare it must have looked by comparison when Daddy first came here more than twenty years ago."

Gracie laughed to herself. Before she came to Biltmore she would have assumed Cornelia was exaggerating when she said hundreds of thousands, but now she took her at her word. If Cornelia said there were hundreds of thousands of trees, there probably were. Gracie smiled appreciatively at the landscape that lay in front of them. "The longer I'm here the more I think that Mr. Vanderbilt and Mr. Olmsted did an amazing job!"

Cornelia had to agree with her. "Sometimes I dream of what it would be like if I lived in one of the bigger cities like my cousins do, in New York City or Newport. All the parties and social events that we would be attending. And the museums that we would be closer to. And, of course, if we lived in New York City, I would be closer to you. But, other than that, it is so much nicer here, where we can go horseback riding almost every day."

Gracie had to agree with her friend. Living in New York City was fine, but it did not compare to this. "Besides, you don't lack for social events, from what I can see."

"No, that's true. They just come to us, almost every night, don't they?"

A servant appeared with two large glasses of icy lemonade and the girls settled back into their chairs enjoying their drinks and soaking in the view. Neither spoke for a few minutes and Gracie thought she might actually doze off enjoying the fresh air and the quiet. But before she could close her eyes too tightly, Cornelia brought her back to the task at hand. "We should dry off our hands and go back to the Library. I really want you to see some of the chapters in the second volume."

Both girls put their tall glasses on a nearby table, drying their hands on the towels that had been conveniently placed next to the tray. Back in the Library they carefully placed the first volume back on its shelf and removed the second one. As they carried it to the table, Gracie grunted. "I do believe this book is heavier than the first one."

Cornelia shook her head. "I think they are actually the same size, I think we just wore out our arms with the first one. Here, let's turn quickly to the chapter on Botticelli. It includes illustrations he made for Dante's *Divine Comedy*. And look, here, what Mr. Berenson wrote of Botticelli, 'He loved to make the line run and leap, to make it whirl and dance.' Isn't that poetic?"

Gracie was already spinning the words around in her mind, *to make the line run and leap and whirl and dance.* "Yes, that is quite lovely. And a beautiful description of an artist's work."

Before they could dwell on Botticelli for too long, Cornelia was moving forward in the book. "You really must see the chapters on Leonardo da Vinci and Michelangelo, too. Those are my absolute favorites; they are rich with information and drawings."

Gracie made herself more comfortable on the stool she sat on, glad they had taken the break on the balcony. As they turned page after page of the beautiful book, she had to agree with her friend, the Renaissance chapters were absolutely the best.

"Doesn't this just make you want to go to Florence and see where all these men lived and worked?" Gracie asked wistfully.

Cornelia acted as if she hadn't heard the question. Her opportunities to travel abroad so far surpassed her friend's that it made her self-conscious. Fortunately Gracie didn't seem like she was waiting for an answer, as she had already turned her attention back to the pages in front of them.

As they finished the book, Gracie could hardly contain her excitement. "I really must thank your father for sharing such wonderful books with me," she said. "I've never seen the likes of these at the New York City Public Library."

Cornelia was fairly certain of that. "They were only written sometime in the last decade. I heard Daddy speak one time of how few of them had been printed. I'm sure he will be happy to have them appreciated. Did you want to get another book now, or are you literate enough for the moment?" With that Cornelia eyed the large chess set across the room and Gracie knew what was coming. "How about some chess for a change of pace?"

Gracie was fairly certain Cornelia would beat her in every game, but she good naturedly agreed anyway. For one thing, it was amazing to actually be able to play with a set as fine as this one. "Sure, let the games begin."

Both girls concentrated on the board in front of them for game after game. Gracie surprised herself by actually winning one of the games. *I'll have to thank Beth for playing with me,* she thought. Before either girl was ready, word came from Mrs. Vanderbilt that dinner preparations were being made.

"Is it really that late?" Cornelia wondered out loud. "Come quickly, Gracie, let's pick out our gowns for this evening."

Gracie willingly followed after her friend. *I'm still enjoying this,* she thought, *though I think dressing up so much for dinner night after night would actually get old at some point.*

# Chapter Nine

Gracie was the only guest that night for a change, and the family sat at the smaller table, near the triple fireplace. Gracie was happy to have a rare opportunity to talk with both of Cornelia's parents. "Thank you again, for allowing me to visit, Mr. and Mrs. Vanderbilt," she started, as the servants carefully laid the first course on the table in front of each of them. Gracie watched her friend carefully, still anxious to make sure she chose the right piece of silverware for each course.

Mr. Vanderbilt answered first. "Thank you for joining us, Miss Gracie. It means so much to Cornelia to have you visit. Sometimes I think she spends too much of her time with stuffy adults."

Cornelia started to protest and he winked at her. "You are welcome to visit us anytime your parents can spare you. In fact, we were hoping you could join us this winter, for our Christmas and New Year's celebrations. After what happened to the *Titanic*, I think we will be traveling abroad in warmer months, at least for a while."

Cornelia jumped with joy at the idea and Gracie chose not to respond to the *Titanic* comment. After thanking Mr. and Mrs. Vanderbilt again for their kind invitations, she decided now, with no other company sharing the table with them, would be a good time to pry Mr. Vanderbilt with some questions about Biltmore.

"Mr. Vanderbilt," she asked quickly, before she lost her nerve. "Cornelia has told me a little about the building of Biltmore, but I would love to hear more, if you wouldn't mind telling me. I find it all so fascinating."

Mr. Vanderbilt looked at his wife and his daughter to be sure that they wouldn't be bored to hear the stories yet again. Seeing slight nods from both of them, he smiled at Gracie. "Well, of course. Anything in particular you would like to hear?"

Gracie grinned. "Oh, any of it. All of it. How you came to build here, so far from the city you were living in, the design of the house, your art collection. Any of it."

"Well," Mr. Vanderbilt took a drink of his wine, "I don't know if our meal will be quite long enough to cover all of that! How about I tell you some of the beginning, and then tomorrow if the weather is bad again, I can meet you girls in the Library and share some more with you then?"

Gracie nodded her appreciation. She loved to hear these kinds of stories. In between the different courses of the meal Mr. Vanderbilt sketched out the beginning of his dream for his estate so many years before. "I was a young man, in my twenties. I had inherited some money from my father and my grandfather."

Gracie laughed to herself. Only Mr. Vanderbilt could describe his inheritance as "some money."

"My older siblings were already building their own mansions in New York City and Newport. But I wanted something different. I had enjoyed the family farm on Long Island, and longed for more space and more land than I was going to be able to get in any of the larger cities. But I hadn't decided where I wanted to build."

Gracie nodded. It was hard to imagine this family being happy in those closed-in places.

Mr. Vanderbilt continued, "After the railroad lines connected New York City to Asheville, many of my friends were visiting this area to enjoy the beautiful mountains and the fresh air. After my father died in 1885, my mother's health was worsening. We visited Asheville at the recommendation of her doctor and we both fell in love with the place. I stood in the window of my room at the Battery Park Hotel and gazed out at the hills and mountains here. That's when I knew this is where I wanted to build my home."

Cornelia giggled at the romanticism in her father's voice. He pretended to glare at her before continuing. "When we returned to the city I immediately contacted Mr. Olmsted and Mr. Hunt. They had both done work for members of the Vanderbilt family and I was confident they could handle what I had in mind."

After what felt like just a few minutes, Gracie looked down, surprised to see dessert in front of her. Had the entire meal really gone by so quickly?

Her mind rewound to the different details that Mr. Vanderbilt had recounted for her, including how his plan for a modest 60,000 square foot home had somehow mysteriously tripled. Yes, she had really listened to him talk about the origins of his Biltmore estate through almost an entire meal.

She was sad to see the meal ending and hoped that she hadn't monopolized too much of the conversation by asking him about it. She looked at Mrs. Vanderbilt and Cornelia and was suddenly confident that they didn't tire of hearing him tell the stories either.

As the servants cleared away the last of the dishes from in front of them, Mr. Vanderbilt promised to continue the stories at a future time. Cornelia jumped up, grabbing Gracie by the hand. "Come along, we can go up to the roof and see the stars before we get out of these elegant clothes."

Gracie dutifully followed her friend back to the elevator and the girls got out on the fourth floor. Cornelia led Gracie to a part of the house she hadn't seen before. As they entered, Gracie thought it looked like a tower room that Rapunzel might have actually enjoyed being kept in. Cornelia waved her hand across it, stating simply, "This is the Observatory Daddy built. Isn't it beautiful?"

Gracie admired the oak paneling and the leather furniture as they walked briskly through the room, taking note that it contained yet another fireplace. She followed Cornelia carefully up the narrow but elegant spiral staircase and out onto a narrow balcony surrounding the room on two sides. The girls made their way carefully from the small balcony to a larger balcony and then onto the roof.

"What a wonderful view of the sky, Cornelia." Gracie looked around with glee. "It must be quite a view of the entire estate as well."

Cornelia smiled at her friend's enjoyment. "I'm sorry we haven't made it up here before. We'll have to come up again sometime during the daytime so you can actually see the property. From here we can see the gardens and the Conservatory, as well as much of the land, of course. It will also give you a closer look at Daddy's gargoyles up here along the edges of the roof. Maybe we can do that tomorrow."

Gracie nodded, hoping so. She had noticed the gargoyles from the ground, and agreed that it would be fun to see them up close. But for now she would enjoy the stars. The rain earlier in the day had cooled the air off beautifully; the air was fresh and the sky was delightful. Gracie could definitely see why Mr. Vanderbilt and his mother had fallen in love with the area the first time they had visited here.

As they raced to see which constellations they could point out first, Cornelia squeezed Gracie's hand. "Thank you for not saying anything about the *Titanic* when Daddy mentioned it in passing earlier. It is still a difficult topic for Mother."

Gracie nodded. She had almost forgotten that the topic had come up during the meal. She had been wondering how they were doing since hearing of the tragedy, and was very glad that she hadn't inadvertently made Mrs. Vanderbilt more uncomfortable.

Cornelia stared out at the stars and spoke through tears. "We came so close to being on that ship, Gracie. So close. Sometimes I wake up in a sweat thinking about it. Just before the *Olympic* was to sail from England my Aunt Susan wired us to please come home early. She made it sound like it was because we had been gone too long, but I think Daddy heard worry in her words. He was actually looking forward to being on the *Titanic's* maiden voyage, but he didn't want to upset her, so he changed our plans."

Gracie rubbed her friend's hands, not knowing what to say. *It sounds like she just needs to talk about it,* she thought sadly as she stood quietly.

Cornelia breathed deeply, as if trying to clear her mind of all that she had heard of the tragedy. "Mother and I were fine with staying in England as planned and sailing on the *Titanic,* but we were also okay with leaving early. The worst part of making the decision to change so last minute was that the best suites on the *Olympic* were already taken."

Even as the words came out of her mouth, Cornelia looked embarrassed. It seemed so petty now to be talking about the suites. Gracie patted her hand again, trying to console her. "I'm so glad your father heeded your aunt's concerns."

Cornelia turned to Gracie, trying to muster a smile. "Me too. But even now, weeks later, Mother grieves for the servant we lost on the *Titanic*."

Gracie was surprised. She hadn't realized that anyone connected to the Vanderbilts had been on the *Titanic.*

Cornelia noticed Gracie's confusion and tried to explain, "Because we changed plans at the last moment like we did, there wasn't time to have all our luggage transferred to the *Olympic*. We each brought only a few trunks with us, and one of Daddy's manservants stayed behind to bring the dozens of other trunks home for us. He sailed on the *Titanic* as originally planned."

Gracie helped Cornelia to a nearby chair, standing close as her friend sobbed.

# Chapter Ten

Refreshed from a good night's sleep, both girls were happy to see good weather again. It looked like a wonderful day for being outside. As soon as breakfast was finished Gracie and Cornelia scrambled out a side door. They chased each other through the Walled Garden, trying not to step on any of the beautiful flowers that were being so carefully tended by the Biltmore gardeners.

When they were both out of breath they collapsed on one of the wooden benches, admiring the flowers closest to them.

Cornelia spoke first. "Isn't it lovely to sit under the arbor like this, Gracie?"

Gracie looked around, trying to figure out who or what an arbor was.

Cornelia pointed around them. "This beautiful area in the middle of the garden with the trelliswork. It's called an arbor.

This is one of my favorite spots. I'm so glad you got to come in the spring, Gracie. And I'm glad you'll be staying long enough to see how the colors change a little from month to month, as the different flowers come into bloom. Daddy's landscaper, Mr. Olmsted, made the original plans for these beautiful gardens and Mr. Beadle helps our gardeners keep things growing when and where they're supposed to."

Cornelia carefully pointed out some of the different flowers to Gracie, who just nodded in appreciation. She always enjoyed looking at beautiful flowers, whether in paintings or in real life, whether she recognized what they were or not. For the moment, she was content with her level of enjoyment of all things growing.

After wandering in and out of the flowers, the two girls climbed up the small hill that overlooked the house, the gardens, and the small reflecting pools. Atop the hill Mr. Vanderbilt had placed a swing for Cornelia and her friends to enjoy. Gracie loved swinging next to Cornelia, looking down at so much of the estate. It was another lovely view of an amazing place, and Gracie couldn't help but wonder how the family could leave it as often as they did.

As they enjoyed the view, Cornelia suddenly yelled, "Race you to the fountains." Suddenly both girls were racing down the hill, towards the closest fountain.

Gracie pulled up as they approached it, but Cornelia jumped right in. "It's okay, Daddy and I used to swim in the fountains all the time. Join me."

Looking around, Gracie cautiously moved closer to the fountain, just in time for Cornelia to splash her in the face.

# Chapter Eleven

A week passed before the weather turned sour again. After breakfast the two girls practically danced to the Library to await Mr. Vanderbilt. Gracie was surprised that Cornelia seemed almost as excited to hear her father's stories as she was. The girls sat down across the chess board from each other. "We might as well get in a game or two while we wait for Daddy to arrive," Cornelia exclaimed.

The girls were just setting up the pieces for a second game when Mr. Vanderbilt strolled into the room. "Oh good, I see you two are enjoying Napoleon's Chess Set."

Gracie was surprised. "As in, *the* Napoleon?" she asked as she pulled her hand away from the piece she had been moving.

Mr. Vanderbilt smiled at her concern, "Yes, that Napoleon. But, please finish your game and then we'll have story time."

Gracie tried to concentrate on her next moves, but was having trouble with her thoughts wandering here and there. She was actually glad when Cornelia won the game quickly.

Putting the pieces carefully back on the board for whomever wanted to play next, the girls quickly crowded around Mr. Vanderbilt.

"I would love to hear more about the building of Biltmore, Mr. Vanderbilt, but would you mind telling us about the chess set first?" Gracie asked in awe. "The entire set is so beautifully made. The ivory pieces feel wonderful in my hand."

Mr. Vanderbilt nodded. "Did you know that Napoleon liked to play chess?"

Both girls shook their heads, as Gracie tried to recall what facts she did know about Napoleon. She had to admit to herself that it was sadly very little.

Before he said more, it seemed that Mr. Vanderbilt was deep in thought, as if trying to solve a most perplexing problem. "I'm sorry girls that my memory isn't better, so I can't tell you for sure, but I think this chess set may actually have been the first Napoleon item that I ever received. I do know that it was a gift for my twenty-first birthday. I had been interested in Napoleon for a few years at that point, in fact, since I had first seen the chess set when I visited the Holland House on the edge of London."

With that pronouncement, Mr. Vanderbilt stopped, as if reconsidering what he had just said. "Well, no, now that I think of it, my very first interest in Napoleon was when I was sixteen. It was on one of my many trips to Europe with my father. We visited Napoleon's tomb. I've been studying him ever since. But, I wasn't telling you about that visit, was I? Have I told you girls about my visit to the Holland House?" Both girls shook their heads, though secretly Gracie wished he would stick to his story about the chess set.

"The Holland House was a favorite place for artists, authors, and philosophers to visit during the eighteenth and nineteen centuries."

Gracie couldn't help thinking that would be a good description of the Biltmore in the twentieth century as Mr. Vanderbilt continued, "There they would be entertained by Lord and Lady Holland. But by the time I visited with my parents, it was Mr. James McHenry that we were going to see. Let me see, I must have been about seventeen years old on that trip. But I digress. Mr. McHenry was an American friend of my parents. I think he also made his money in the railroads."

The two girls looked at each other, trying not to outwardly groan. Neither could see how any of this was connected or how any of it related to Mr. Vanderbilt obtaining the chess set.

But they sat quietly, hoping the pieces of the puzzle would come together as Mr. Vanderbilt continued. "Let's see, how did that all go? Mr. McHenry lived on the edge of the estate property while the Hollands were alive. After their death he seemed to have become somewhat of a caretaker for the property for the new owners, some distant cousins of the Hollands. He loved to show people around and share stories of the property and the home."

The girls were having difficulty keeping a straight face as Mr. Vanderbilt looked their direction. "Oh, you want to hear about the chess set?" he said in mock surprise.

Mr. Vanderbilt continued, "Apparently Napoleon was a passionate chess player, though I've heard he wasn't particularly good at it."

Gracie thought, *Well, I guess Napoleon and I have something in common.*

"Mr. McHenry informed me that Lady Holland had the ivory chess pieces made especially for Napoleon while he was in exile towards the end of his life, after hearing that chess was his favorite before-dinner pastime. She sent him the chess set along with boxes of books and candies."

Gracie and Cornelia were really confused now. How had a gift from Lady Holland to Napoleon had made its way to Mr. Vanderbilt? But they didn't have to wait too much longer before he continued, "After Napoleon's death the chess set was bought in an auction by a Mr. Andrew Darling. Apparently Mr. Darling was Napoleon's undertaker and he acquired numerous items from Longwood House, including several mahogany tables and Napoleon's specially made cane seat chair. And, of course, the chess set."

The girls looked like they didn't know whether to cry or laugh. Cornelia finally braved the question they were both thinking, knowing they were in danger of sending Mr. Vanderbilt on another rabbit's trail in the process. "What was the Longwood House, Daddy?"

Mr. Vanderbilt stopped momentarily, as if finally trying to figure out how much of this story the girls really wanted to hear. "The Longwood House was Napoleon's home when he was in exile there on the island. Apparently Mr. Darling had come to St. Helena from England to furnish the home for Napoleon and then never left. Mr. Darling seemed to have been quite taken by Napoleon, and purchased the various Napoleon articles at the auction. Or he may have just been a shrewd businessman. After Darling's death, his family sent the articles on to England to have them auctioned there. I believe Mr. McHenry paid a tidy sum for the chess set at that point, desiring to return it to Holland House.

*Okay,* Gracie told herself, *I can now see how the chess set got from Lady Holland to Napoleon and back again, but*

*I still don't know how Mr. Vanderbilt ended up with it.*

Mr. Vanderbilt finally got to the part of the story the girls had been trying to wait patiently for. "On my first visit to Holland House, Mr. McHenry showed me around the estate quite a bit. Since I was so interested in its history and architecture, he shared many of his stories with me. The chess set, along with his descriptions of Lady Holland and Napoleon writing letters back and forth for so many years, really strengthened my fascination with Napoleon."

"And?" Gracie and Cornelia blurted out together, looking at each other and giggling.

"And, when I returned to London on my own a few years later, I made a point of returning to Holland House. Mr. McHenry was in the process of disposing of some of the marvelous literary works in the Holland collection, since for some reason the new owners weren't interested in maintaining a 10,000 volume collection." Looking around the Library at a room that was purported to hold only half of Mr. Vanderbilt's own 20,000 book collection, Gracie could see why Mr. Vanderbilt didn't understand that sentiment.

"Mr. McHenry had also republished a twenty-nine volume set about Holland House, its owners, and its numerous guests that I made arrangements to purchase from him. At that time Mr. McHenry presented me with the chess set as a gift. 'For your twenty-first birthday, I can hardly think of a more appropriate present. May it always bring you great enjoyment,' he said. And that, young ladies, is a very long-winded explanation of why I have Napoleon's chess set sitting here in my library."

Gracie had enjoyed the not-so-short story about the chess set, but she still looked forward to hearing more about Mr. Vanderbilt building his home. "So once you decided you wanted to build a home near Asheville, what did you do?"

Gracie and Cornelia gathered closer to Mr. Vanderbilt, who relished sharing the stories with the two girls. "Well, after I had made the initial decision, I had agents start purchasing land in the area for me. And to think, I started with only nine acres. In fact, it was nine acres right here in the area where the house is situated. I knew I would want more than that, but it wasn't until we had bought up over 120,000 acres that I realized how much more."

Both girls were trying to imagine that initial purchase. Gracie remembered Cornelia telling Gracie that the house itself sat on four acres. Gracie almost laughed trying to think of a house as big as the Biltmore sitting on land that was only nine acres. *I just don't think that would have worked very well,* she told herself.

Mr. Vanderbilt continued. "As I was telling you ladies earlier, I made arrangements to meet with Mr. Hunt and Mr. Olmsted almost as soon as I returned to New York."

"You've seen their portraits upstairs, right?" Cornelia asked her friend.

"Oh yes, the two beautiful large portraits by John Singer Sargent in the second floor hall."

Cornelia nodded. "Mr. Sargent is one of my favorite modern artists. Have you also seen the portrait he did of Daddy? It's my favorite portrait of all those that he did."

Gracie nodded and Cornelia continued. "Mr. Sargent is known

throughout Europe and the United States for his great painting skills, and Daddy still got him to come here to do those portraits. Isn't that fun?" Cornelia didn't really expect an answer, and went on, "Of course, that was before I was born, so I didn't get to meet him."

Gracie tried not to laugh, looking at Cornelia's pitiful face. Mr. Vanderbilt glanced at his daughter. "Well, I believe Mr. Sargent is living in England these days. Shall we look him up the next time we're that direction?"

Cornelia eyed her father, trying to decide if he was being serious. "Could we, Daddy?"

Gracie tried to keep her groaning to herself as she tried to imagine having such a conversation with her own father. She couldn't even bring up a good image of her or her father speaking those words. She struggled to keep the green-eyed monster of jealousy under control as she listened to more of their outlandish conversation.

# Chapter Twelve

It was another week or more before the girls had an opportunity to sit down with Mr. Vanderbilt again. There had been another evening without guests and he had invited them into the Billiard Room after dinner to try their hand at pool and billiards. Gracie looked around in surprise at the dark walls and the beautiful animal prints that graced each side of the room. She had never been in this portion of the house. Cornelia leaned over and whispered to her, "The bachelor's wing, usually reserved for the male guests."

*No wonder we've never been over here before,* Gracie thought as she tried to mimic the way Cornelia and Mr. Vanderbilt held the pool cues. But she found herself more interested in the beautiful sticks with their inlaid ivory than the game itself.

After they had played just a couple of games, they all sat in very comfortable leather chairs. Mr. Vanderbilt started to tell the girls about his shopping trip to Europe with Mr. Hunt, soon after the planning of Biltmore had begun. "While we were shopping we visited various chateaus in France to get ideas for how we wanted to build the house. I think that's when the original plan started being enlarged. We also visited several estates in England to get ideas for the interior."

At that moment he glanced down at his pocket watch. "Look at the time girls, we are going to have to bring this conversation to an end. More family stories will have to wait for another time."

The girls giggled again and scooted out of the Library. Gracie thought to herself, *well, little by little I'll learn more about Biltmore.*

~^~

Gracie was surprised that they had actually had two evening meals within a week's time where she was the only guest. As the delicious salads were being served at the second one, Gracie turned towards her gracious hostess. "Mrs.

Vanderbilt, what is your favorite part of traveling? Or your favorite place to travel to? If you don't mind me asking."

Gracie was surprised how quickly Mrs. Vanderbilt responded. "I would have to say Paris is my absolute favorite place to travel. Of course, I suppose it doesn't hurt that that's where Mr. Vanderbilt proposed to me, and where our wedding took place."

Mr. Vanderbilt winked at his wife and she continued, "But it also helps that of all the languages I speak, French is one of the few that I speak as well as I speak English. Before our engagement I had lived in Paris for many years with an older sister. It's such a lovely, historic city that also happens to be a little romantic – with its boulevards, the parks, and of course, the Louvre."

Gracie and Cornelia exchanged glances, both enjoying the descriptions of Mrs. Vanderbilt's beloved Paris. Gracie wondered if she would ever manage to visit a place so wonderful.

She watched Mr. Vanderbilt smile at his wife before he interrupted her. "After Edith accepted my proposal of marriage, I promptly set to having her room here at Biltmore decorated in the classic

French Louis XV style; I wanted her to feel right at home. As queen of my heart and queen of our estate, I wanted her to have a room that made her feel royal."

Mrs. Vanderbilt smiled the sweet regal smile Gracie had seen so many times. She was sure that Mrs. Vanderbilt was the closest thing to royalty that she would ever meet.

Mrs. Vanderbilt picked up the story. "The room was absolutely stunning, of course, with the gold silk wall coverings and the deep purple velvet draperies. But George had bowled me over with everything at the estate, long before I got to that part of the house."

Mr. Vanderbilt grinned like a mischievous school boy, Gracie thought, glad she had brought up the subject. Cornelia just looked on in quiet delight, clearly happy to have a friend who enjoyed the family stories as much as she did. Mr. Vanderbilt interrupted his wife again, explaining, "I had designed the entire house and property with the hope that I would someday cease to be the country's most eligible bachelor, and become instead the country's happiest husband."

It was his wife's turn to smile. She winked at her husband and turned her attention back to the girls. "After so many years abroad, traveling throughout England and France for much of my life, and then throughout Spain and Italy on our honeymoon, I thought I had seen the world's most magnificent homes. It wasn't until our carriage came up the approach road and then stopped across from this house that I started to realize what a magnificent home I was moving into."

Mr. Vanderbilt picked up the story again. "It was a beautiful day when we arrived home from the honeymoon. We were welcomed to the estate by the largest horseshoe of flowers you can even imagine."

Cornelia elbowed Gracie, "Remember, I showed you a photograph of that?"

Gracie nodded. She recalled wondering how anyone could possibly have had that many flowers, but now that she had seen the many gardens on the estate, it wasn't so difficult to imagine.

Mrs. Vanderbilt continued, "I was so thrilled by the reception that I got out of the carriage and walked under the horseshoe, amazed to see that both sides of the road were lined with workers and their families who had come to welcome us home."

Gracie glanced at Mr. Vanderbilt, who was clearly proud of the way his workers had greeted them. "Each of the workers carried something related to their job on the estate, a hammer, a hoe, a rolling pin, that type of thing.

Edith interrupted him again, "And the children, George, they were so precious. I didn't know at that time how long it would be until we had our own little blessing, but I determined right then that I would help see to the needs of the children living here on the estate."

Gracie knew that Cornelia had always felt that even though she was an only child, her mother's love was shared so many different ways. In fact, when the girls had first met, Gracie sensed that Cornelia felt like her mother had cared too much for other people's children. But Gracie suspected that now that Cornelia was a much wiser eleven-and-a-half-year-old, she could probably see that her mother had the capacity to care for so many others and still love her dearly.

# Chapter Thirteen

Gracie's attention turned back to Mrs. Vanderbilt as she continued the story of her arrival. "After greeting everyone and hugging as many of the children as I could, George convinced me to get back in the carriage for the several mile drive up to the front of the house. When we drove in front of the house, he had the carriage driver stop so I could see the house from the far side of the front lawn, just like you first saw it, Gracie. I don't know about you, but when I first saw it, I felt like I had been transported across the Atlantic back to Europe."

Mr. Vanderbilt broke back in, continuing his portion of the story. "I'm glad I succeeded in my meager attempts at creating our own blend of a French chateau and an English manor house."

In spite of her best efforts at good manners, Gracie almost spit her lemonade all over the plate in front of her at Mr. Vanderbilt's use of the word "meager." She was pretty sure that nothing a Vanderbilt did could be described as meager, particularly this Vanderbilt or this house.

Cornelia put her hand in front of her face and giggled at her friend's response. Mrs. Vanderbilt looked quickly at Gracie to make sure she wasn't choking on something. Seeing the sparkle in both girls' eyes, she picked up the story. "After Mr. Vanderbilt carried me over the threshold of our not-so-meager home, he graciously showed me only the highlights of the home."

Cornelia interrupted her mother, "Which rooms did he start with, Mother? No, let me guess. The Library, the Tapestry Room, and the Banquet Hall."

Mrs. Vanderbilt nodded her head, not surprised that her daughter had guessed the exact rooms. "Your father took me to each of those, excitedly pointing out his favorite books and paintings, and then telling me about collecting the lovely sixteenth century Flemish tapestries. After all that, he escorted me to the most beautiful room in the entire house – mine."

Gracie glanced back at Mr. Vanderbilt, seeing that he was clearly excited, even after all these years, at his wife's reaction to the room he had so carefully designed for her. She continued, "Much like you girls did on Gracie's arrival day, we agreed that the grand tour of the rest of the house could wait a day or two until I had recovered from our trip to Asheville."

Mr. Vanderbilt continued, "I didn't want to tire her too much too early on. Besides, I knew she would want her strength for the events that were yet to come that day."

She smiled. "Just when I didn't think there could be more, there was. That evening we walked out onto the roof balcony. I felt like I was on top of the world. Below us I could hear the band playing and see a line of men marching with torches. Soon the torchlight was joined by bonfires lighting up distant hilltops. And all of that was followed by the most amazing fireworks show I have ever seen in my life. We stood at the top of the world, laughing and listening, clapping and cheering. It was a most exciting time."

Mr. Vanderbilt continued, "My employees had gone all out in welcoming my bride. When we finally tore ourselves away from the magnificent view from the roof, we made our way down to the conservatory where the doors and windows had been opened up. We enjoyed refreshments among the employees until after midnight."

Mrs. Vanderbilt sat silent for a few minutes, enjoying the memories. At last she spoke again, "There was a brief moment that evening when I wondered what I had gotten myself into, but it has been an amazing experience. I don't think I could have been happier anywhere else in the world."

Mr. Vanderbilt squeezed her hand. "Not even in your beloved Paris?" he teased.

"Not even in Paris."

The talk of Paris reminded Gracie of the question she had asked earlier, realizing they had only gotten as far as Mrs. Vanderbilt's answer. "What is your favorite place to visit, Mr. Vanderbilt?" she asked as a servant placed a delicious-looking chocolate dessert in front of her.

"I'm afraid I don't have an answer quite as quickly as Mrs. Vanderbilt did. I've had the privilege of traveling to so many places for most of my life – from the Middle East to the Far East, from Northern Africa to Europe. I have really enjoyed almost every trip."

Just as Gracie thought he was refusing to answer the question, Mr. Vanderbilt continued, "But that's not the type of answer you're looking for, is it young lady? If I had to choose one place, I would have to say that Venice, Italy has been one of my favorites."

Gracie laughed to herself that he had still caveated his answer with the "one of his favorites" phrase. But at least he had given an answer. "Why Venice?" she pried.

"It is a unique city, built on the water such as it is. The small canals that go throughout the city, most of which connect to the Grand Canal, are so much fun to explore. I could spend hours walking through the narrow streets or being taken by gondola through the canals." He laughed and continued, "Yes, I could definitely spend hours doing those things, because I have."

Cornelia interrupted excitedly, "I've seen a photograph of you in a Venetian gondola, Daddy."

He laughed. "Yes, I would imagine you have. The Grand Canal ends near the Doge's Palace, one of the most unique buildings I have ever seen. Like the rest of the city, it is a fabulous blend of Byzantine and Gothic architecture. That's probably one of the things I like about Venice – it is a great blend of east and west. When I stood in the large piazza there, looking out at the lagoon, I imagined Marco Polo heading east from there with his uncle and his father – heading out on the adventure of a lifetime."

Gracie thought to herself, *Mr. Vanderbilt, I think you have already experienced the adventures of several lifetimes,* but she kept the sentiment to herself. She would certainly never want to be rude to her host or hostess. Yet, it was difficult not to think longingly of the traveling the Vanderbilt family did so much of. She longed to have adventures of her own – whether of the Marco Polo variety or the Vanderbilt style.

Mr. Vanderbilt continued, "Art and architecture have fascinated me around the world since I first traveled with my parents as a young boy. One of the unique artistic elements in Venice is the mosaic work. It is beautifully done and very different than you will see in most other parts of Europe."

Gracie smiled at the enthusiasm in Mr. Vanderbilt's voice. She had never doubted, since first meeting the Vanderbilts, that they enjoyed art at least as much as she did. In fact, a mutual appreciation for art was what had drawn the two girls to each other when they had first met two years earlier. Neither had previously met another ten-year-old with similar interests.

So Gracie was not surprised to hear Mr. Vanderbilt mention the art and architecture of Venice as contributing to it being one his favorite places to visit, but for the life of her she couldn't figure out why she might have guessed that. Cornelia must have sensed her questioning herself because she quickly leaned over and whispered to Gracie, "The large painting on the ceiling in the Library was originally done for one of the many Venetian palaces along the Grand Canal."

"That's right," Gracie exclaimed, a little louder than she had planned, "the ceiling fresco. I knew there was a Venetian connection here someplace."

Mr. Vanderbilt smiled before correcting her, "Well, the ceiling painting, that is. It's not actually a fresco. Frescos don't do well in Venice because of the constant humidity there. This ceiling painting was originally done on thirteen smaller strips that were able to be peeled off the ceiling there. That's why we were able to bring it here and reuse it. We would not likely to have been able to do that had it been an actual fresco."

Gracie smiled. *Yes, that makes sense. I had wondered.* "Well, it is a beautiful painting, Mr. Vanderbilt. I'm glad you were able to move it."

"I am too, Gracie. I was in Venice enjoying the beautiful palaces along the canal when my guide quickly pointed out one where the owners were going through some hard times financially. He had heard that as a result there might be some valuable artwork available from the owners at a reasonable price. As you can tell, he was correct."

Mrs. Vanderbilt had been listening to her husband's descriptions of Venice and finally spoke up. "I had never traveled to Venice until our honeymoon. But George had beguiled me with stories of its beauty, too. I can tell you that it is every bit as remarkable as he describes."

Gracie smiled but then realized that dinner had come to an end and she hadn't been able to ask Cornelia about her favorite place to travel. Thinking it was a conversation that would have to wait until a future time, she was surprised to hear Mrs. Vanderbilt addressing one of the servants, "I think we will be moving our after dinner conversation into the Library. Could you bring us some coffee there please?"

The girls looked at each other with excitement as Mr. Vanderbilt took each of them by the arm. "Come along ladies, we are waiting to hear answers from both of you to Gracie's probing question."

# Chapter Fourteen

As they skipped along to the Library, Gracie found herself perplexed. What could she offer as an answer that would mean anything to world travelers such as the Vanderbilts?

As they made themselves comfortable in the Library, Cornelia leaned over to Gracie again. "Relax, Gracie. This isn't a test. There's not a right or wrong answer. I'll go next so you have more time to think of your answer."

Gracie squeezed her friend's hand. How did Cornelia always seem to know what she was thinking?

As soon as everyone was settled, Cornelia spoke up excitedly. "I think my favorite place to visit was Germany. I thoroughly enjoyed our recent trip across Germany, especially when we were in Berlin. We motored our way across the country, staying in such a variety of guest houses. I had forgotten what a beautiful country Germany was until that trip. And there seemed to be castles everywhere. It was fun to see so many castles, though I think none compared to our very own castle, Daddy."

Gracie smiled. Cornelia had sent her many letters from Germany and it had always sounded like a place she would want to visit. *Maybe,* she thought wistfully, *just maybe, I'll be a world traveler someday too.*

Mrs. Vanderbilt nodded her head, agreeing with her daughter. "That was a fun trip. Remember the lovely accommodations where we had to walk through the family's kitchen to get to our rooms? They were so embarrassed, but we absolutely loved staying there."

Mr. Vanderbilt laughed. "Yes, I think we turned a few heads on that trip. But I would have to agree with both of you, that trip was a lot of fun. Well, Gracie, I think it's time for you to answer your own question. What is one of your favorite places to travel to?"

Gracie didn't know why this seemed like such a hard decision to make; it wasn't like she had traveled to very many places from her home in New York City. "Well, of course, I like traveling here, to

Biltmore, a lot. But I have also really enjoyed traveling to the City of Washington. Getting to see the capital of our country was such a thrill to me. To stand in front of the White House or President Washington's Monument, to ride a street car around the National Mall. Each of those just excited me in a special way that I can hardly explain."

Without coordinating it, each of the Vanderbilts started applauding Gracie and her answer. Mrs. Vanderbilt reached over and hugged her quietly commenting, "I have not spent near as much time in the City of Washington as I would like, but I think you are absolutely right. It is a wonderful and special place. As much as we have traveled abroad, it is hard to compare what we have seen and done overseas to what we have seen and done right here in our own country."

Mr. Vanderbilt sipped the last bit of his coffee. "I concur. Thank you again, Gracie for starting us off on a wonderful discussion tonight. But it is getting late and we should all call it a night soon. We have another busy day ahead tomorrow, I'm sure."

Quick goodnights were said and Gracie headed to her room to get out of the beautiful gown Cornelia had lent her for the evening. *It's a good thing Anne is always available to help me out of these things,* she thought. *I don't know how I would manage that feat by myself.*

As Gracie passed a mirror in the hallway, she looked at herself again. *This gown is not as elegant as many of the other ones I've borrowed from Cornelia, but I think I like it best of all. I think Cornelia said this one was homespun cloth, too, from local seamstresses, rather than the imported materials they so often wear. I will have to ask her about that sometime.*

# *Chapter*
# *Fifteen*

Even though she had been up late the night before, Gracie found herself waking early the next morning. As she lay in bed thinking of all the wonderful things she had already done and seen since arriving at Biltmore, she thought again of the beautiful engravings Mr. Vanderbilt seemed to have everywhere in the house. *I've grown up walking through the rooms of the Metropolitan Art Museum, enjoying paintings from the last several centuries from around the world, but I've never seen this many engravings. I wonder how and why Mr. Vanderbilt has collected so many.*

Decidedly awake now, Gracie sat up. It was time to go exploring. Since it was so early, it was unlikely she would run into any of the other guests, and she threw her robe on over her pajamas, suddenly having the urge to see some of the prints up close.

Strolling out of the room quietly so as not to awake Cornelia, she peered both ways. Seeing only a stray servant or two who seemed more interested in their own tasks than the wanderings of a young guest, she stepped boldly out. At that moment she decided her quest would be to see as many pieces of Mr. Vanderbilt's collection of engravings as possible during the rest of her stay at the estate.

*I guess I can start my hunt in the hallway on the other side of the sitting room,* she thought. *We've walked down it numerous times, but I've never really slowed down to even look at the many prints there; we always seem to be rushing by them to get to one place or another.*

Slowly Gracie worked her way down the hallway, wondering to herself what must be involved in making such stunning artwork. Gracie realized that she recognized many of the artists whose work had been turned into engravings – she had spotted Dürer and Rembrandt, as well as several by Raphael. But there were several artists that were less familiar to her. *I would like to make a list of artists to go back and study more about,* she thought.

Gracie continued to enjoy the prints as she worked her way down the lengthy hallway. She had almost reached the end when she realized someone was standing nearby. Startled she turned around, almost bumping into Mr. Vanderbilt, who was watching her with interest.

"I see you are looking at in my prints, Gracie. What do you think?"

Gracie was more than slightly embarrassed to be standing in the hallway dressed in her pajamas and robe, especially to now find herself talking to Mr. Vanderbilt. But to her surprise he seemed not to notice her attire. He was focused exclusively on the artwork in front of them.

She finally managed to muster the courage to answer him. "I've practically grown up around artwork. But I have really only seen sculptures and paintings before this, not etchings like these. They are absolutely beautiful."

Mr. Vanderbilt smiled. He was clearly happy to have his artwork appreciated. "Well then, I hope you take the time while you are here to explore the house enough to see more of the other prints."

"Yes, sir, I would like that very much. I had noticed the etchings when I first arrived, but I hadn't really looked at them very closely."

Pleased with her interest, Mr. Vanderbilt clarified "Some are etchings, but there are also woodcuts, aquatints, and photogravures. These architectural prints have to be some of my favorites."

Gracie nodded in agreement. "I've seen dozens of your prints throughout the house, but I am certain I have not seen most of them. Do you have any idea how many prints you own, Mr. Vanderbilt?"

Mr. Vanderbilt smiled at her enthusiasm. "I have lost count, but I believe there are somewhere between fifteen hundred and two thousand prints throughout the house."

Gracie tried to remember if she had noticed even a fraction of that number. "I have seen and enjoyed paintings by several of these same artists, but I actually find the more monochromatic treatment in the prints to be quite stunning."

Mr. Vanderbilt looked pleasantly surprised at Gracie's comment. "I must agree. And as much as I like paintings, that is one of the things that has drawn me to prints over the years. And they just seem to fit in well with any décor and color combination, wouldn't you say?"

Gracie's mind did a quick trek through the richly decorated rooms of the house that she had seen. "Yes, I would say that you could safely hang the prints anywhere."

"As I indeed have. Some of my favorites are actually going up and down the stairwells. Be sure to look for those."

"Yes, I will certainly do that. Thank you."

Mr. Vanderbilt bowed. "I should let you get back to your observations. It is time for me to join Mrs. Vanderbilt for breakfast in the Oak Sitting Room. Do let me know later if you have any questions." With that he was gone as quickly as he had arrived.

Gracie looked down in embarrassment at how she was dressed. *What would my mother think? I guess next time I want to walk the halls of Biltmore early in the morning, I better put some real clothes on.* Gracie carefully examined the last few prints in the hallway and then hastened back to her room. *I will need to pay more attention to the walls as I go through this amazing house.*

# Chapter Sixteen

Gracie sat in front of the mirror trying not to frown. Even after weeks at Biltmore she still struggled to accept this particular reality. She watched as Anne carefully brushed out her long dark hair. Gracie bit her lip. *I'm perfectly capable of brushing my own hair,* she thought.

But Cornelia had insisted that that's not the way it was done. It was proper to have it done by a servant. Period. *Proper?* She thought disdainfully. *What's proper about not being able to brush out my own hair every morning?*

Gracie turned her focus to the mirror, trying not to be obvious that she was watching Anne's face. Anne looked to Gracie to be just a few years older than herself and didn't appear to mind the task. In fact, Gracie was fairly certain the young woman was humming to herself. Gracie tried to relax. At least Anne always seemed to be around when she had to change clothes so many times each day.

Gracie thought of how often she found herself changing clothes every day and almost laughed out loud. *I think I wear more clothes in a day when I'm visiting Cornelia than I do in a week when I'm at home. And I can't even get in and out of so many of these outfits by myself. I wonder how many times I'll get dressed today?*

*I'll be back up here changing into riding clothes before we hit the trails, and then into another outfit for lounging around, and another for afternoon tea.* Gracie had planned to count, but was quickly losing track. *And then of course there's the long, extravagant dress I'll have to change into for the formal dinner at 8:00. And most likely another outfit after that before bed.*

Gracie realized that Anne had finished the job of brushing her hair. She was waiting patiently for Gracie, somehow seeming to understand that Gracie had been lost in her own thoughts.

"Thank you, Anne."

"How would you like your hair put up today, Miss Gracie?"

"However you would like to do it, Anne. Just something simple, that won't be too much work for you."

Gracie wondered why they seemed to have this conversation every day. Anne had clearly been instructed to abide by Gracie's every wish, but Gracie wasn't that particular. The last thing she cared about each morning was what her hair was going to look like. *No, that's not true,* she thought. *I probably care less about which outfits I'm going to wear.*

It had taken a couple of days after their arrival for the girls to work out some sort of a system, but Gracie had finally convinced Cornelia that she should just inform both lady's maids of the outfits for the day. *Most of what I'm wearing are Cornelia's clothes anyway,* she thought again.

Anne picked up a lovely spring dress for Gracie to see. "I hope you like the dress Miss Cornelia chose for you to wear this morning."

Gracie's eyes sparkled as she looked at the dress. "Oh Anne, it's lovely. I don't think I've seen this one before."

Anne nodded. "I believe it's another one of the homespun dresses that Mrs.

Vanderbilt bought recently for Miss Cornelia. I thought you might like it."

Gracie allowed Anne to help her into the dress, and stood in front of the mirror smiling as Anne fastened all the buttons in the back.

"Thank you, Anne, for helping me again. I'm sorry to be so much trouble with all these changes each day. And to have to call you to come down here for all of this."

Anne shook her head and Gracie sensed that she was trying not to laugh. "Miss Gracie, my room is not that far from here, just up on the fourth floor. And you are no trouble at all. I'm not sure when the last time was that I helped a guest who required less attention than you."

Gracie smiled. "My mother would be glad to hear that."

# *Chapter*
# *Seventeen*

Gracie rolled over in her bed, dismayed to be awake so early again. She could tell from the light barely coming through her window that it was way too soon to be getting up and getting ready for the new day.

But after trying unsuccessfully to go back to sleep she gave up and sat up in bed. She was glad that Cornelia had given her the bed closest to the door and that she had finally succeeded in getting Anne to leave one of the simpler dresses in the room so she might actually be able to dress herself in a situation like this.

Anne had initially balked at the idea, insisting that Miss Gracie could ring for her at any time. But Gracie had held her ground, deciding that if she awoke early again, she wanted to be able to explore the mansion in proper attire, without first summoning Anne.

Gracie quietly pulled the dress on over her head, trying not to disturb the sleeping Cornelia. She ran a brush through her hair. *Wow, I'm glad I haven't forgotten how to do this, it's been too long since I did it myself.*

Glancing in the mirror Gracie realized Anne would insist on doing her hair again later, but at least she would be presentable for her early morning excursion this time around.

Gracie made her way as quietly as she could down the hall to a set of back stairs. She had discovered a back way down to the Library the last time she and Cornelia had been playing hide and seek in this part of the house. Gracie laughed to herself as she made her way quietly. *Cornelia has the only house I've ever been in where we have to set boundaries for our game. It wouldn't be much of a game to play Hide and Seek in this entire place - the seeker could never win!*

Opening the small door in front of her, Gracie entered the Library from its second floor. Standing among the books, so many books, and so close to the large ceiling painting made her almost giddy with excitement. Her eyes made their way slowly around the entire room before she could even bring herself to move. She finally made her way around it, wanting to see the books at this level closer up.

*I had never realized how many different languages Mr. Vanderbilt had books in. I wouldn't be able to read many of these. I will have to look for the books in English or French,* she realized, glad she had at least been learning a second language. *I can tell that Mr. Vanderbilt has a great appreciation for history,* she thought as she continued by shelves and shelves of historical books. *He has quite the taste for good literature as well. Maybe I could read one of his Dickens novels when I have some free time. Maybe, though, it may take the rest of the summer,* she thought, *as much as we do around here now that school is out.*

Gracie found a novel by Charles Dickens that looked interesting. *It looks like it's about the French Revolution,* she thought as she paged through *A Tale of Two Cities. That might be interesting.*

Gracie glanced around. No one had entered the Library since she had arrived. She slowly made her way down the small spiral staircase and sat in one of the big comfortable chairs near the fireplace. *I can see the clock on the mantle above the fireplace from here, so*

*I can keep an eye on the time. It wouldn't do if I wasn't back in my room when Anne showed up to help me get ready for breakfast.*

As Gracie got comfortable she pondered how glorious the room must feel and look with a fire blazing in the fireplace. *I wonder how many fireplaces this house must have.* She quickly found herself transported to Paris through the pages of the novel. *What a wonderful place to visit Paris must be,* she thought, remembering how fondly Mrs. Vanderbilt had spoken of her time there. Gracie chided herself, *I shouldn't spend too much time thinking of that, or I'll get jealous again. Where was I in the book?*

Gracie had been reading along at a fairly rapid pace, enjoying the story, when she realized someone else had joined her in the Library. She looked up, pleased to see Mrs. Vanderbilt standing nearby. Gracie arose, to greet her hostess. "Mrs. Vanderbilt, I see you are also looking for early morning reading."

Mrs. Vanderbilt smiled at their young guest and sat down in the chair closest to Gracie. "Yes, and I see you have found Mr. Vanderbilt's collection of

Dickens. I am partial to that one, with its setting in France."

Gracie nodded. "It's the first of Mr. Dickens' novels that I've actually read, other than his *Christmas Carol,* of course."

Mrs. Vanderbilt smiled. "I didn't mean to interrupt your reading time. I just came down to find some light reading myself."

Gracie glanced to see what page she had been on, and then quickly closed the book. "No, it's fine. I can read it later. If you have a few minutes, I would love to converse with you before we both head back to our rooms for breakfast. I haven't had much time to talk to you since my arrival."

Mrs. Vanderbilt nodded her head. "My daughter is so happy to have a companion, that she certainly monopolizes your time. But, it has been good for her to have someone her own age to occupy her this summer. We appreciate your willingness to go along with her ideas. I hope that it hasn't been a burden for you."

Gracie laughed in spite of herself. "No, ma'am, it has not been a burden at all. I have quite enjoyed the various activities we have done so far this summer. Many of them were new to me. I had never been horseback riding or swimming before. We don't have much opportunity for those in New York City."

Mrs. Vanderbilt nodded. "That's one of the many reasons we live here in North Carolina, rather than in the big city. We all enjoy the great outdoors and the various activities that are available as a result, though I think horseback riding may be the favorite for all of us. Did you enjoy the horseback riding, Gracie?"

"Oh, yes. It took me a little bit of time to be willing to try. The horses all seem so big when you get that close to them, that I was more than a little afraid. But Cornelia waited patiently until I was willing to get on. We went for quite a ride once I got used to it. I think we may have ridden over the entire estate."

Mrs. Vanderbilt hated to disagree with her young guest, but she finally shook her head. "I doubt that I've seen the entire estate yet, Gracie. I've been told it would take an entire week to ride over the entire acreage. I haven't been inclined to try."

Trying to take in how large the estate really was, Gracie sat still for a few minutes. She found herself contemplating how any one family could ever own so much. Turning back to Mrs. Vanderbilt, one of the large blue and white ceramic bowls caught her eye. "I've noticed a number of items in the Library and in a few other rooms that are distinctly Asian. Does your family travel often to Asia?"

Mrs. Vanderbilt glanced around at the lovely items. "Oh yes, the Ming Dynasty fish bowls. Unfortunately Cornelia and I have never had the opportunity to travel beyond Europe. But Mr. Vanderbilt traveled to Japan soon after starting the building of Biltmore. He returned with many, many boxes of items that he had purchased while he was there. These are a few of the numerous items that he brought home from China and Japan."

Gracie looked around the room again wondering if she could ask Mr. Vanderbilt about that trip. It was hard for her to even imagine something as exotic as traveling to Japan.

Mrs. Vanderbilt seemed to sense Gracie's desire to know more. "I would be happy to tell you a little more about the trip if you would like. I would prefer you not bring the topic up with Mr. Vanderbilt."

Gracie was surprised but nodded her ascent. Who was she to question Mrs. Vanderbilt's request?

Mrs. Vanderbilt thanked her and continued, "I appreciate your willingness to agree without asking more questions. I will explain why in a bit. But first, a little more about his trip to Japan. Mr. Vanderbilt was invited there for the Emperor's birthday celebration."

Seeing the surprise on Gracie's face, she continued, "Emperor Meiji's birthday was always a national holiday with a large public ceremony at the Imperial Palace in Tokyo. The Emperor worked very hard during his reign to open Japan to western ideas after more than two centuries of isolation. For his fortieth birthday he made a concerted effort to invite representatives from a wide variety of western countries, including, of course, the United States."

Even with all of that Gracie was having difficulty understanding why Mr. Vanderbilt would receive an invitation. Mrs. Vanderbilt sensed her surprise.

"You're having difficulty imagining a Vanderbilt receiving such an invitation, I see. One of the things the Emperor was working hard to do was improve the transportation within his country, particularly the railroads. My understanding is that he requested someone from the United States with connections to our railroads. From that very short list, George Vanderbilt's name rose to the top."

*That makes sense,* Gracie thought, still very surprised.

"George Vanderbilt took his cousin, Clarence Barker, with him on many of his travels, including his trip to Japan. In fact, George and Clarence had just returned from a trip to Spain when he received the invitation. Even though they were exhausted from their previous trip, they couldn't pass up the opportunity to go the Far East. I believe they traveled west from here, stopping to see Mr. Hunt in Chicago where he was supervising the final touches on the Administration Building at the World's Columbian Exposition.

Then it was off to Yellowstone and on to California to finish their trip to Asia. I understand that they had a fabulous time. George has told me stories of his visit, of all that he saw and did while they were there. In addition to visiting many of the Japanese touristy-type sites, they also did quite a bit of shopping – visiting many antique dealers while they were there."

Gracie wished that she could hear more of the stories herself, from Mr. Vanderbilt himself. But she had promised Mrs. Vanderbilt that she wouldn't ask, and whether she understood the reasons or not, she would obey her hostess' wishes.

But Gracie didn't have to wonder about the reasons much longer. Mrs. Vanderbilt continued, "Your ability to sit there perplexed but not saying anything is quite remarkable for a young lady your age. Sadly, George's cousin Clarence died here at Biltmore just a few months after George's mother died. The death of his mother was quite difficult, of course, but she had been ill for some time, and at her age it wasn't totally unexpected. But Clarence was quite young, and his illness was very short. Even after all these years, George does not seem to have gotten over Clarence's death. I prefer not to have topics brought up that may help his grief return."

Mrs. Vanderbilt's request was now making some sense. "Yes, of course. I would not want to make Mr. Vanderbilt uncomfortable. Thank you for sharing with me about his trip to Japan."

Just then Gracie noticed the time on the mantle clock. "Oh dear, Mrs. Vanderbilt, we will be late for breakfast if we don't hurry back to our rooms."

Mrs. Vanderbilt smiled, picking up the book she had chosen upon entering the room. "Yes, I will see you girls at breakfast shortly. It's a good thing we are both capable of getting ready for the day quickly."

Gracie smiled back at her, took her selection and rushed back towards the stairs at the top of the Library.

~^~

After many more weeks of fun inside and out, Gracie found it hard to believe that her visit at Biltmore was coming to an end. She had enjoyed the summer with the Vanderbilts even more than she had anticipated, her biggest difficulty deciding what she had enjoyed the most. The long talks almost every evening after dinner with Cornelia probably topped her list. But the countless horseback trails she had grown comfortable on and her growing appreciation for art were both close to the top. She was certain that her future trips to the Metropolitan would be even more enjoyable than those of the past.

Mr. Vanderbilt had business in New York City to attend to, so her return trip had been timed to coincide with his trip. Cornelia accompanied them to the Asheville Train Depot, and sadly said her goodbyes to both of them. Both girls hoped it would not be too many months before they were able to meet up again.

Gracie settled once again into the luxurious seat of the Vanderbilt's private car, watching with interest as the chef approached Mr. Vanderbilt with a menu of their meals for the next two days. *Yes,* she thought, *I could see how someone could get used to this type of comfort.*

# Chapter Eighteen

Gracie returned to New York City just in time to start school again. She found it hard to try to get back to her normal routine after living so many months with the Vanderbilts. But she threw herself into her daily life – her chores at home and her school work, and tried not to think too hard about her time away.

Every once in a while she found herself remembering the travels, the books, or the long talks with Cornelia. If she had a few extra moments at the end of a long day she would find herself lying on her bed, examining the ceiling, and daydreaming about someday being a world traveler. Then she would remind herself that her destiny had not been to be born into a family like the Vanderbilts, and she would roll over and remind herself to be thankful for who she was and what she did have.

Each week when the family made their Sunday treks to the Metropolitan, she would stand at the top of the stairs looking out at Central Park, thinking of her carriage ride with Cornelia. Then she would enter the museum determined to make the most of each visit. Sometimes she could convince Beth to walk through the galleries with her. She tried not to compare Beth to Cornelia as they went. But it was clear to her that Beth liked art more on the level of Cornelia – wanting to pick out one piece and really focus on it.

The letters from Cornelia came faithfully. They told of the new dogs that the family had recently received – great big St. Bernards that Cornelia couldn't wait to show Gracie. And she spoke of the authors who were becoming regular guests. The letters were always fun to read, but always made Gracie miss Cornelia and Biltmore just a little more.

~^~

The invitation came unexpectedly. The Vanderbilts had mentioned the possibility of Gracie returning at some point during the winter following her first visit, but that visit hadn't worked out. Suddenly word had come that the family was postponing their next travel plans to after the new year. They would be delighted to have Gracie join them for the Christmas holidays.

Gracie held the invitation in trembling hands. She was almost afraid to show her parents. She so desperately wanted to go, but to be away from home at Christmas time? She had never done that before and wasn't sure she was ready. As Gracie held the invitation, trying to decide what do, her younger sister came into the room. Beth gasped when she saw the beautiful card in Gracie's hand. "Where did that come from, Gracie?"

Gracie hesitated before answering. She was still deciding if she even wanted to ask her parents, and here her sister was, pestering her. "It's an invitation from the Vanderbilts. They've invited me to join them for Christmas this year."

Beth looked like she couldn't decide whether to smile or cry. Instead of doing either, she just hugged her sister. "Have you asked Mama and Papa yet?"

Gracie shook her head. But before she could say anything, her sister was running off to the kitchen. Gracie could hear her exclaiming, "Mama, come see Gracie's beautiful invitation."

Gracie groaned. Any possibility of just dismissing the invitation had just vanished with her sister. In just a few moments her mother was standing in front of her, drying her hands on a dish towel, with a look of anticipation.

Gracie cleared her throat, still trying to decide what to say. *Well,* she thought, *here goes nothing.* Gracie handed her mother the invitation. "The Vanderbilts have invited me to join them for Christmas." She hesitated, still not sure what she wanted to do even if she had a choice.

Mama looked over the card and then looked carefully at her eldest child. "Well, are you taking them up on their generous invitation?"

Gracie looked at her, tears welling up in her eyes. "I would love to, Mama, but to be away from home on Christmas. I just don't know."

Mama hugged her and spoke compassionately, "We would miss you, dear, of course, but you are almost fourteen years old. And Cornelia has never had siblings to share Christmas with, like you have always had. I think it would mean so much to her to have you there."

Gracie hugged her mother tightly. "Oh, Mama, thank you for understanding. I really would like to join them."

After confirming with Papa that Gracie could make the trip to Biltmore over the holidays, word was sent back to the Vanderbilts that Gracie would accept their gracious invitation. Mr. Vanderbilt sent word that they would make all of the travel arrangements for Gracie. Some of their extended family would be traveling from New York City in the middle of December. They would send a car to take Gracie to the train station so that she could travel by train with Cornelia's cousins in their private railway car.

The two weeks between the arrival of the invitation and Gracie's trip seemed on the one hand to drag on forever, and on the other to speed by too quickly. Finally the time for packing rolled around. Gracie pulled out the trunk she had taken on her previous trip to Biltmore.

Beth stuck her head into the room while Gracie packed. "What you doing?"

the younger girl asked in her sing-songy voice.

Gracie made space on the bed for Beth to sit. "I'm packing for my trip to Biltmore next week. Do you want to watch? Just don't touch things please."

Beth smiled appreciatively and moved further into the corner of the bed, giving plenty of distance between her and her older sister's things. "Will you be gone long this time?" she asked, with clear concern in her voice.

Gracie stopped what she was doing and walked over to her sister, giving her a reassuring hug before answering. "Well, Beth, just traveling to and from Biltmore takes so long, that yes, even if I only stayed a week or two, it would certainly seem to you as if I was gone a long time. I think I will be staying past New Years, so it will be several weeks."

Beth's lower lip came out in a pout and Gracie continued, "But remember the nice present I brought you the last time I returned? The beautiful scarf that the Vanderbilts had sent for you."

Beth brightened a little. The scarf was now one of her favorite things to wear in the cold New York winters. "Will you bring me something again?" she asked expectantly.

"Well," Gracie paused, not sure how to answer. She didn't want to give her sister false hopes but also didn't want her to be as upset about her upcoming departure. "I can certainly try. I will talk with Cornelia about it when I arrive and see what we can come up with."

Beth seemed satisfied with her answer and Gracie went back to considering her packing. She really didn't need a whole trunk to take her things to Biltmore, but the extra space had come in handy for her last return trip. Gracie finished piling up the few clothing items she had decided to take and approached the small bookcase in the corner of her room.

Beth broke the silence again. "Do you really read when you are visiting your friend?"

Gracie laughed at the way her sister asked the question, as if it was the strangest idea she had yet heard. "Yes, I read sometimes when I'm there. Mr. Vanderbilt has the most exquisite library you can even imagine. During my last visit, Cornelia and I curled up in there sometimes with good books, usually when the weather was too hot or too wet to go outside." Gracie thought longingly of the thousands of books to choose from just in that one room in the large house, to say nothing of the books located in the other places throughout the home.

Beth broke into her thoughts again. "Why don't you just read Mr. Vanderbilt's books while you're there, then?" she asked, clearly confused.

Gracie smiled. "I do read some of his books when I'm there. I'm just looking for a few to take with me for the trip there and home again. The train ride takes two day each way. I won't be traveling with Cornelia this time and I can only look out at the beautiful scenery for so long."

Beth seemed satisfied and sat back to watch her sister again. "I am so jealous that you get to travel so much, Gracie. It just isn't fair."

The hurt in Beth's voice made Gracie stop. She returned to her sister and hugged her again. How strange that she had been trying hard not to be jealous of the Vanderbilts' world travels, and here her own sister was jealous of her travels. Gracie tried to reassure her, "Your time will come, Beth, I'm sure of it.

When you are older, you will get a chance to travel outside of New York City too."

Beth looked skeptical. She was only two years younger than Gracie and she knew how many trips her sister had made even by the time she was her own age. She leaned back against the wall and pouted again.

Gracie frowned. She really hadn't considered what her own family members thought of her trips away. *I guess if I was in Beth's place I wouldn't think it was fair either,* she thought sadly. She would definitely have to bring something home for her younger siblings, one way or another.

Gracie moved all of her carefully placed things quickly to the empty trunk that stood waiting expectantly at the side of the bed. Then she jumped up on the bed next to her sister and kissed her on her check. "Please don't look so glum, Beth. If I could take you with me you know I would."

Beth hugged her older sister and went back to watching, but Gracie noticed that the frown had softened slightly. She promised herself to try to pay a little more attention to Beth in the remaining time before her departure.

The talk with Beth had reminded Gracie that she needed to think of a Christmas gift to take for Cornelia. They had agreed the previous summer to limit their gift exchange to something small. Gracie knew she could never afford to give Cornelia anything that she couldn't buy herself. She struggled with what she could bring that would seem special to someone who really had everything.

The following Sunday when her family visited the art museum again, Gracie watched the artists that were situated throughout the museum with their easels and their paint supplies, copying a variety of masters. *That's it,* she determined. *I will finish the landscape I started when I returned home from Biltmore.*

Gracie hadn't realized when she had started painting the landscape how much of a resemblance it had to the mountains around Biltmore. *I think that would make an acceptable Christmas gift for Cornelia. It is certainly not something she will already own.*

Working on the painting in her spare moments helped the time before her trip go more quickly. When the painting was completed, she allowed it to dry completely and then wrapped it carefully to place it in her trunk. Now all she had to do was wait for the time to finally arrive for her next departure.

# Chapter Nineteen

Gracie straightened her long skirt, wishing again that the trip to Biltmore didn't take so long. *But, it sure is out there a distance,* she thought, *so of course, it isn't a quick journey.* With that, Gracie settled back into the seat of the railway car. *I can hardly complain about a lack of comfort. I might as well get some rest – once I arrive at Biltmore rest will be sparse. No matter how much time Cornelia and I have spent together, we never seem to run out of things to talk about – often late into the night.*

Gracie shifted again in her seat, smiling at the thought of what awaited her. Cornelia had been telling her how nicely decorated her home always was for the Christmas holidays. Gracie giggled out loud, in spite of herself. It was still hard to think of a house as big as Biltmore as a home, but in spite of its grandiose size, that's really what it was.

*Even if I probably couldn't count the number of my family's homes that would fit inside of it, it is a home, too,* she reminded herself. Gracie remembered her promise to herself to bring something home for Beth and the younger kids. *I will need to talk to Cornelia about that early on, so I don't forget.*

~^~

Gracie and the Vanderbilt relatives were met in Asheville by two luxurious carriages. The weather had worsened during the latter part of their train ride, and Gracie was beginning to think the trip would never end.

She wasn't completely surprised that the carriages didn't pull up in front of the main doors of the mansion as they had the first time she had visited. Instead, they pulled past the front doors, towards the stables, stopping one at a time in front of a side door that Gracie had never noticed.

As she exited the carriage she marveled at the area that had been built over that portion of the driveway. *Mr. Vanderbilt and Mr. Hunt did seem to think of everything, didn't they? I wonder why I never noticed this particular door when I was here before.*

As Gracie was ushered into the house she realized she was standing in the Bachelor's Wing, in front of Mr. Vanderbilt's Gun Room. *Oh, that explains it. Cornelia and I didn't exactly spend much time at this end of the house.*

Cornelia came running out of the Banquet Hall just as Gracie and the cousins were being helped out of their coats. Practically ignoring her relatives, Cornelia greeted Gracie like a long lost friend and took her friend by the hand ushering her further into the house.

"Gracie, you've lost weight since I saw you a year and a half ago. I think Mother's dressmaker will have to take in some of my dresses in order for you to wear them this time. But come along, I've been waiting to show you the countless Christmas decorations. Come, let's go to the Banquet Hall first."

Dutifully Gracie followed after her friend, trying to see all the trees and poinsettias as they walked; they seemed to be everywhere. It was hard to imagine what Cornelia wanted to show her so badly. But when Gracie stepped into the large room, all doubt was erased. In front of her stood the largest Christmas tree she could have even imagined. "Oh

Cornelia, this is the loveliest tree I have ever seen. Look at all those ornaments. There must be thousands."

Cornelia stepped forward towards the tree, her eyes sparkling. "I don't know, shall we count them?"

Gracie giggled. "No, I don't think that would be a good use of our time together. We'll just assume there are more ornaments than rooms in your house, but less than books in your father's library."

Cornelia grinned. "Yes, I'm fairly certain we could assume those things. But, come, I have something else I want to show you. I need your help with something."

With one last look at the amazing tree with its stunning ornaments, Gracie followed obediently after Cornelia. She struggled to think what else Cornelia could possibly have to show her.

But this time Cornelia led her away from the elaborate decorations and upstairs towards the bedrooms. Soon Gracie found herself near what she thought were Cornelia's parents' rooms. *I wonder what we're doing over here.*

Rounding one more corner Cornelia pulled Gracie into a small room and switched on the Edison light bulb. Gracie found herself surrounded by stacks and stacks of toys, toys of all shapes and sizes. "What is all this, Cornelia? I don't understand?"

"This, my dear Gracie, is what I need your assistance with. Each Christmas my mother buys presents for all of the children who live on the estate. I thought this year you could help me wrap them. Would you mind?"

Gracie looked around the room, trying to estimate how many toys and other gifts must be present in the room. *How did Mrs. Vanderbilt even purchase all these?* She wondered. "Oh, no, I wouldn't mind at all, Cornelia, that sounds like fun. Maybe we could sing Christmas songs while we worked on them."

"I was hoping you would agree to do it with me. We can come back later today and get started. But come along, now I want to show you some more of the Christmas decorations in the house before it's time for afternoon tea.

# Chapter Twenty

Gracie sat in the Banquet Hall awaiting the next course of the sumptuous meal. It was hard to imagine any place in the world being lovelier. Even though the house had been built with central heating, a roaring fire filled the triple fireplace on one side of the room. And the immense Christmas tree filled the other side. During dinner Gracie looked at the tree intently. It seemed to reach far up towards the high ceiling of the room – taking its unique ornaments with it almost out of sight. She was quite certain that Jack, of Jack in the Beanstalk fame, would be quite at home in the top of its tall branches. She looked towards the small balcony overlooking the room, almost expecting Jack and the giant to appear there. Instead more green garlands and red ribbons greeted her.

To one side of the tree sat a large table with the countless gifts that

Cornelia and Gracie had lovingly wrapped for the families of all the workers on the estate. On the other side a small table sat with a much smaller stack of gifts – the gifts from the family members to each other. Gracie had managed to keep a piece of the wrapping paper back from one of the gift wrapping sessions with Cornelia. She had then succeeded in wrapping her own gift and adding it to the pile when Cornelia wasn't looking.

As a delicious smelling plum pudding was placed in front of her, she found herself worrying again over whether or not Cornelia would like her gift. *Well, it's too late now,* she reminded herself. *I can't exactly retrieve it from the pile.* With that she tried to turn her attention back to the wonderful meal they had all been enjoying together.

After dinner had been completed and dishes cleared away, Mr. Vanderbilt leaned back comfortably in his chair. He had a cup of steaming apple cider in one hand and a copy of Dickens' *Christmas Carol* in his other.

"Next on the agenda is a dramatic reading of our favorite Christmas story," he announced.

"Bah, humbug," a few family members playfully responded.

Gracie had always enjoyed the evening story times or read-alouds during her previous visit and was happy to see that the Vanderbilts also enjoyed Dickens' little Christmas story at this time of year. *It's hard to imagine Mr. Vanderbilt reading it as well as Papa does,* she thought, *but I would imagine he'll be a close second.*

Gracie had been concerned about spending Christmas Eve and Christmas Day away from her family, but so far the day had been quite delightful.

Mr. Vanderbilt took another sip of his cider and then cleared his throat. "As has been our tradition here at Biltmore for the last eighteen years, we will read Dickens' *Christmas Carol* and then exchange gifts." With that he proceeded to read in a deep and animated voice that reminded Gracie of her own father's reading voice. He held the small book as he read it, though Gracie was quite certain that he actually had much of it memorized.

Even though she remembered hearing the story for most of her thirteen years, Gracie sat mesmerized as

Ebenezer Scrooge met one spirit after another. She smiled and laughed with the rest of the family when he changed his ways at the end.

As the story wound to its inevitable conclusion, Gracie was reminded of a discussion she had overheard the previous year between two adults who were discussing whether Dickens was actually preaching an anti-capitalist message in his little book. Watching Mr. Vanderbilt read the story so forcefully, Gracie had to doubt it. Here was the youngest son of one of the most capitalistic families in America thoroughly enjoying the story.

*No,* Gracie told herself, *I think Dickens' message is more like the essay Mr. Carnegie wrote about the need for philanthropy amongst the richer families in society. And I see that attitude often in the many things Mr. and Mrs. Vanderbilt do to help their community and the families on their estate,* she thought as she looked again at the larger stack of presents near the tree.

Just then her attention was brought back to the middle of the long banquet table where Mr. Vanderbilt had just tapped lightly on a nearby wine glass.

"And now for the Christmas Eve gift giving."

Gracie watched as two sharply dressed servants took turns retrieving gifts from the small pile and then handing them to Mr. or Mrs. Vanderbilt. Mr. Vanderbilt would announce the name of each gift's recipient as well as the person who had given the gift. A small gift was soon brought forward and he announced, "For Miss Gracie from Cornelia."

One of the servants brought the gift around the table to Gracie who opened the gift with trembling fingers. *I've never opened a gift with quite this many people watching,* she thought nervously.

As Gracie removed the lid from a small white box, she took out a small, beautifully made, silver bracelet. She gasped, "I have never seen anything quite so lovely. Oh, thank you, Cornelia."

Cornelia beamed at her friend's delight and helped Gracie slip the beautiful bracelet onto her wrist. *I don't think I own anything that I could ever wear this with at home, but I can certainly enjoy it while I'm here,* Gracie told herself.

As the gift giving continued Gracie worried again about how inadequate her own gift would seem by comparison. At last the time came and Mr. Vanderbilt carefully handed Gracie's gift to a servant to present to Cornelia.

Gracie looked on with growing unease as Cornelia carefully unwrapped the painting. She held it in front of her at arm's length, carefully taking in the beautiful artwork in front of her. It was only after she had admired it for a few moments that she realized that it was Gracie's own signature carefully placed in the lower left corner of the painting.

"Oh Gracie, it's so lovely." With that, Cornelia finally turned the painting around so that the others in the room could also admire it. "I never knew you painted, Gracie."

Cornelia carefully handed the painting to her nearest cousin to hold as she jumped up to hug Gracie. "It's the best gift I've ever received, Gracie. Thank you so much."

As Cornelia sat back down both girls realized that the painting was being passed carefully around the table. Oohs and ahs could be heard from around the room as it traveled. When the painting stopped in front of Mr. and Mrs. Vanderbilt, Gracie could feel her cheeks reddening. *This man has seen and collected some of the best art from around the world and here he sits holding my little attempt at a landscape.*

As Mr. Vanderbilt passed the painting on around the table, he spoke. "Gracie, I knew you had a real appreciation for art but I never dreamed you also had such a talent for art. Some of us are not that creative."

As he paused Gracie could barely contain her laughter. This from the man who had created the most magnificent home in the country, if not the world. *No, she thought, I'm fairly certain he can't claim not to be creative.*

Mr. Vanderbilt continued, "Have you been studying long? Do you plan to continue? You clearly have a talent."

Gracie wasn't even sure how to answer those questions. Hadn't she spent her entire life studying the masters at the Metropolitan? Beyond that she had no formal training and no plans at the moment to receive any. She just had supportive parents who had allowed her to dabble in paint for as long as she could remember.

"I've never had any formal lessons, nor do I think we can afford them any time soon. My parents allow me to spend any extra money on painting supplies and I paint when I can, but that's really it."

With that Gracie stopped, not even sure what else she could say. She looked over at her friend, who had finally gotten her gift back from its trip around the table. Gracie was happy that Cornelia seemed to be genuinely pleased with her gift.

As the servants brought around cups of Wassail punch for everyone, Gracie looked around the room happily and whispered to herself, "As Tiny Tim said, God bless us, everyone."

The following afternoon both girls were allowed to deliver the gifts from the larger pile to Mr. Vanderbilt as he presented them to his many servants and their families. Mrs. Vanderbilt sat comfortably next to him, greeting each person by name, and clearly enjoying watching the unwrapping of the gifts she had so carefully chosen.

Refreshments had been laid out on tables in several of the first floor rooms and the employees and their families circulated cheerfully among the rooms –

on the one day each year that they were the guests rather than the servants.

After several hours all the gifts had been delivered and most of the food had been consumed. As the servants dispersed to enjoy the rest of their day off, the family members moved to the Library where Gracie noticed that another blazing fire greeted them. Until it was time to dress for Christmas dinner, they sat in the Library and enjoyed singing Christmas carols together.

It hadn't occurred to Gracie until that moment that the house had no Music Room. She wasn't exactly an expert in mansions, never having stepped foot inside any except for this one, but it still seemed odd to her. It seemed that music rooms usually came up in stories involving the homes of rich people.

After a lovely time of singing, Cornelia and Gracie and the others headed towards their rooms to change, Gracie asked her, "Is there a reason there is no Music Room at Biltmore? It doesn't seem like a lack of interest in music can possibly be the reason. I've seen pianos in several rooms throughout Biltmore. I've heard your father talk about the opera enough times. And clearly many of you have beautiful voices."

Cornelia looked around, as if to make sure she wouldn't be overheard by anyone except Gracie. "Mother was telling you about Father's traveling companion, his cousin Clarence, right?"

"Yes, she mentioned him when she was telling me about their trip to Japan."

"Uncle Clarence was the family musician. He had gone to school for music and was quite talented. He was helping Father design the Music Room when he died. Father couldn't bring himself to finish the room after Clarence's sudden death. He closed up the room and it's been closed ever since. I don't think anyone is ever allowed into it."

Gracie nodded, thankful again that she had asked Cornelia the question, rather than her father.

"I'm so sorry."

"It's okay. It was a long time ago. I never knew him, or my grandparents either. Father's mother was the last of my grandparents to die, and that was four years before I was born."

Suddenly Gracie thought of her own grandparents. She had just sort of taken them for granted. All four of them were a regular part of her life, with one set living in the city, and one living close enough that they could visit regularly. She had never considered just how special that was.

Realizing they had made it to the hallway outside their rooms, Gracie hugged her friend and then opened the door. Anne awaited her, along with the most beautiful Christmas dress Gracie had ever seen. She said a little prayer of thanksgiving for family and friends and tried to turn her attention back to the holiday they were celebrating. "Unto us a child is born, unto us a king is given," she found herself singing softly as she sat down for Anne to brush her hair out and arrange it for the evening festivities. Gracie was quite sure that she had already experienced the most special Christmas Eve and Christmas of her life.

# Chapter Twenty-One

Gracie and Beth stepped into the foyer of Biltmore. Gracie was pleased to see that, even after so many years, it appeared that much of the property and house were unchanged. She noticed that Beth was still having trouble taking it all in and Gracie tried to remember what she had felt like the first time she had visited Biltmore. Sympathetically she allowed her sister some time to admire their surroundings.

A servant stepped out of the room just as the girls entered. Gracie didn't realize she had gone to fetch Miss Cornelia until Cornelia came running into the room. "Gracie, you've made it for my party. I wasn't sure you would get the invitation in time to make travel arrangements." Cornelia almost squeezed Gracie hugging her so hard. "And this must be your sister, Elizabeth."

When the bear hug was over, Beth reached out her hand, "Beth will do just fine, Miss Cornelia."

Cornelia giggled at the formalities, "And Cornelia will do just fine also." Refusing the hand she went from hugging Gracie to hugging Beth. Stepping between the two girls she took each of them by the arm. "This way ladies, to the balcony. There is still enough daylight for us to enjoy the view from there for a little while as we catch up."

As they passed a call box, Cornelia paused, requesting three glasses of lemonade. Beth was still trying to observe more of the house as they headed towards the balcony, but Cornelia wouldn't slow down. "Gracie can give you a grand tour of the house later, Beth, don't worry. And if the weather is pleasant during your stay, we'll have to take a swim in the new outdoor pool. Mother had it added recently."

With that, Cornelia turned anxiously back to Gracie. "How long has it been? How did we let the time go by so long without getting together? It's just been too long, hasn't it?"

Beth got comfortable in her seat, enjoying the view she had heard about for so many years. She had no difficulty seeing why it had shown up in so many of her sister's paintings. But, before long, tired from their travels, she found her eyes drifting closed. The fresh breeze from the nearby hillside felt refreshing.

Gracie looked at Cornelia, trying to remember the last time they had been together. It seemed like just yesterday, but it also seemed like a lifetime ago. "I think the last time I was here was the winter before we both turned fourteen, the Christmas just before..." Gracie caught herself, not sure whether she wanted to bring up Cornelia's father so soon.

But Cornelia smiled her familiar smile. "It's okay, Gracie, that was a lifetime ago. We were almost fourteen, and here you are for my twenty-first birthday. I cannot tell you how good it is to see you again. I want to know everything you've done for the last seven years, just everything. But first, please tell me about Paris. I haven't been there in years. Someday I dream of moving to Paris or London and being an artist or a writer. But, regardless, I was so excited to hear that you were living in Paris now, Gracie."

Gracie smiled, trying to figure out where to start. Even starting with Paris would be difficult. "The last time I was here, so many years ago, your mother mentioned that she still had connections in Paris from when she had lived there, and your father still knew people involved in the art community there. They both said that I should let them know when I was finished with my regular studies in New York."

Gracie sat back, soaking in her favorite view before she continued. She had now painted landscapes throughout France, but was sure none were more beautiful than this, the first landscape she had ever painted.

"When I arrived that last Christmas I had no thought of actually pursuing painting, it was just something I did for fun. But by the time I left I could hardly think of anything else. All the way home I wondered how I would broach the subject to my parents and what they would think."

Cornelia smiled at the thought of her parents helping propel Gracie towards her career. "I'm so glad they were open to the idea, Gracie; it would have been such a waste of talent otherwise."

Gracie nodded. "I'm confident your parents had something to do with their acceptance. They had to warm up to the idea, of course, but they never came right out and said no, which was a good start."

As Gracie thought back to those years, she tried to remember when the idea of her going to Paris had actually become a reality. "My father's biggest concern was me going to Paris alone. And as long as a war was waging worldwide, it was simply out of the question anyway."

Cornelia had only met Gracie's parents a few times, but she had no trouble seeing those as insurmountable stumbling blocks. "But, obviously you did go to Paris, so what changed his mind?"

Gracie smiled. "By the time the Great War had ended, it was finally time for Beth to start traveling. Beth agreed to accompany me and suddenly my parents were willing to let us go."

Cornelia hugged her friend's hand. "I'm so excited for you. And you will need to tell me more about how Paris is these days and how the art is going. But I should show you to your rooms and we can figure out what costumes you two are going to wear for the costume party tomorrow night. Mother will be dressed as a peacock. And I'm wearing the most wonderful outfit – that of a Renaissance page. The black velvet costume is simply stunning. Oh, and wait until you see the Venetian Sedan chair that mother sent for so that I could arrive at the party in style."

The girls got up, and followed Cornelia as she led them across the house. Her mood seemed to change ever so slightly. "We closed up part of the house after Daddy's death, Gracie, so you won't be in your usual room, but I think you will enjoy this one too. I put you and Beth in the two rooms closest to mine. Come along and I'll show you to our rooms. One of the joys of being in the Bachelor's Wing is that my favorite staircase is in that portion of the house. Do you remember it, Gracie, it goes all the way from the basement to the roof?"

Gracie smile again. "Yes, of course, we used to play hide and seek at that end if there were no guests present in the house. Some of your father's prints that

I really loved are hanging in that stairwell. Rembrandt, as I recall."

Immediately, Gracie wished she hadn't mentioned Mr. Vanderbilt's artwork. It now seemed painfully clear to her that Cornelia was not holding up as well since his death as she was pretending.

Cornelia slowed her pace and lowered her voice a little. "I missed having you here, Gracie. So much has changed. We've reduced the number of servants significantly as Mother has tried to keep the estate running smoothly. It has been so much for her to keep up with. I don't think either of us realized how much Father did in managing the estate. Mother has hired a lawyer, a Mr. Adams, I believe, that helps take care of things. She seems relieved to have his assistance. Miss King, the head housekeeper, stayed a few years after Father's death, but she left us a few years ago and moved to Florida."

Cornelia finally took a breath and Gracie wondered if there was something helpful or gracious that she could say. Instead she hugged her friend, who continued in a somewhat more cheery tone, "But Anne is still with us, the dear darling, so I've arranged for her to be your lady's maid again. So that will be just like old times."

Gracie smiled in spite of herself. She wondered if she would be able to convince Anne that she could do her own hair this time around!

# Author's Note

Of course, George, Edith and Cornelia Vanderbilt were real people, who really lived exciting and exotic lives in and out of Biltmore. Gracie is completely fictional, though I did try to make her character very believable.

The descriptions of the Vanderbilt family, their home, and their travels are generally quite historically accurate, with the limited exceptions noted here. The explanation of how Mr. Vanderbilt got invited to the Emperor's birthday party, how he received Napoleon's chess set, and why he didn't finish the Music Room are all suppositions, but they are plausible explanations based on what we do know about each of those.

Most of the chess set story is historically based – the set was made for Napoleon by Lady Holland, it was bought at auction by Mr. Darling, and it was given to Mr. Vanderbilt by Mr. McHenry.

What is unclear is how the chess set made it from Mr. Darling to Mr. McHenry.

I also took a little creative license with the portion of the story about the Vanderbilts' personal railway car. George did own one of those – but only from 1891 to 1904. When it was damaged by a fire he sold it rather than repairing it, and the family traveled by passenger train or their personal automobile after that.

George had an immense library – owning more than 20,000 books – many of which he had indeed read. He kept a log of the books he read each year, averaging eighty-one books per year for his entire adult life.

The Vanderbilts did change their mind about traveling on the Titanic at the last minute for unknown reasons. Some have suggested that they were concerned that their trip home might be delayed because of an impending coal strike, and others that they changed their plans to travel with friends.

Mr. Vanderbilt's cousin and traveling companion, Clarence Barker did die young – he was in his early thirties.

Sadly, Mr. Vanderbilt also died young – he was 51; his only child,

Cornelia was almost 14 when he passed away. Mrs. Vanderbilt did close up much of the house after his death, and she did put on quite a "coming out" party for Cornelia's 21st birthday. Cornelia did dress as a Renaissance page for that party, but her mother didn't actually wear the Peacock costume until a party the following year. (Costume parties were a big part of the lives of most well-to-do families during this era, including the Vanderbilts.)

# Historical Timeline

**1862** George Vanderbilt is born on Staten Island

**1872** George makes his first trip to Europe with his parents

**1873** Edith Stuyvesant Dresser is born in New York City

**1879** George visits Holland House in Kensington, England

**1880** The new, larger Metropolitan Museum of Art opens

**1880** The railroad reaches Asheville, North Carolina

**1883** George receives the Napoleon chess set

**1884** Hunt and Olmsted work together on the family mausoleum

**1888** On a trip to Asheville decides to build a country home there

**1889** George begins purchasing acreage in Asheville

**1890** Construction begins on the Biltmore

**1891** Vanderbilts' private railway car, the *Swannanoa*, is built

**1892** George attends Emperor Meiji's 40th birthday celebration

**1895** Biltmore is mostly finished (George moves in in October, officially opening the house on Christmas Eve)

**1896** George's mother dies

**1896** George's cousin Clarence dies at Biltmore (at age 31)

**1897** George and Edith both attend Queen Victoria's Diamond Jubilee Celebration in London

**1898** Edith and George are married in Paris

**1900** Cornelia is born at Biltmore

**1907** George sells much of the art he inherited from his father

**1912** Vanderbilt's servant, Edwin Wheeler, perishes on *Titanic*

**1914** George dies in Washington, D.C.

**1921** The Coming of Age Masquerade Party for Cornelia

# About the Author

Catherine wears many hats these days – from mother to teacher, to historian to author. One of her favorite genres to read and write is historical fiction, and she has authored numerous historical novels and short stories. Her writings have included several novels about Leonardo da Vinci and a short story about the "monuments' men" and their work in Wuerzburg, Germany.

Catherine has traveled extensively - throughout North America, Europe and Asia. Her many trips have included following the Lewis and Clark Trail in 2005 with members of her family and volunteering at Jamestown during the four hundred year anniversary in 2007. On a trip back to Panama (her birthplace) in 2008 she started her "Horsey and Friends" series, which she has continued during recent school trips to Washington, D.C. and Virginia. Throughout her travels and her teaching she has found much inspiration for her writing.

Made in the USA
Columbia, SC
29 January 2023

11183763R00091